UPHEAVAL

D1596803

Also by Susan J Crockford

Fiction

EATEN: A Novel

Non-Fiction

The Polar Bear Catastrophe That Never Happened

Polar Bear Facts and Myths

Polar Bears: Outstanding Survivors of Climate
Change

Rhythms of Life: Thyroid Hormone and the Origin
of Species

UPHEAVAL

A short novel

by

Susan J Crockford

Copyright © 2020 by Susan J. Crockford

All rights reserved. No part of this book may be reproduced
or transmitted in any form or by any means, electronic or
mechanical, including photocopying, recording, or by any
information storage and retrieval system, without permission
in writing from the author.

Published in 2020 by Susan J. Crockford

ISBN 978-0-9917966-3-2

Cover design by Nigel Sutcliffe

Preface

Inspiration for this story came from discussions I've had over the years with friend and geology colleague Jim Baichtal about earthquakes and tsunamis. Jim lives on the coast of Southeast Alaska, I live in Victoria on the southern coast of British Columbia—both are active earthquake and tsunami zones. After writing about polar bears and the Arctic for more than fifteen years, sea ice is often on my mind and one day I got to thinking what would happen if a tsunami hit when the ocean was covered with ice. I discovered that very little was known because it happened so seldom but what little science had been done on the phenomenon was pretty frightening. In the course of my research, I also found out about the tsunami that had devastated the Burin Peninsula of Newfoundland back in 1929 and realized I had the core concept for a science-based fictional story to follow *EATEN*, the polar bear attack thriller I published in 2016 (and yes, there are polar bears in this one too).

This new story is shorter than *EATEN*, technically a 'novella' rather than a full-length novel. I hope readers won't be too disappointed at the length but I feel it suits the topic. It's taken much longer than I'd hoped to get it finished—distractions to writing, as many others have discovered, have been far too plentiful since late March due to government responses to that blasted coronavirus. I also had to deal with a family tragedy (not a Covid 19 death but definitely a consequence of Covid 19 restrictions) that tested my commitment to writing fiction. However, I'm pleased with the result. Most importantly, I think it adequately answers my initial question with as much detail as most people would care to have: I have imagined an ice tsunami disaster that is scientifically plausible. My story is based on scientific facts and some worst-case scenario possibilities no one has yet contemplated. Of course, the final responsibility is mine and if I've got something really wrong, it's on me.

The names are fictitious, and the people are not meant to represent anyone living or dead. The name of 'Izzy' for one of my main characters is a small tribute to my geologist friend Bob Carter, who explained via email several years before he died why he and his wife wanted to use this name for the dog they bought—but in the end called him something else.

I want to thank my family for their enthusiastic support for this second foray into fiction, especially my sister Cairn Crockford, a professional historian and fiction lover who served as editor. Nigel Sutcliffe drew the cover image and Andrew Montford, who edited my 2019 polar bear science book, *The Polar Bear Catastrophe That Never Happened*, provided the map at no cost on behalf of the *Global Warming Policy Foundation*. I am most grateful to all of them.

For an introduction to the world of polar bears on the east coast of Canada in fictional format, *EATEN* is suitable for teens as well as adults and is available in paperback and ebook formats (including pdf) through a number of online retailers. For critical polar bear background past and present, see *The Polar Bear Catastrophe That Never Happened* and my blog www.polarbearscience.com. My other books, including a polar bear science book for children, can be found at my author website, www.susancrockford.com. For social media connections, see https://twitter.com/sjc_pbs.

Prologue

by Nick Oliver, Corner Brook, Newfoundland 2046

This is a unique first-person account of the greatest tsunami disaster ever to hit a North American shore.

Duff Gillies was my grandfather's best friend from his Dingwall days on Cape Breton Island, Nova Scotia, an area on the north end the locals call "North of Smokey" ('Smokey' being both a ski hill and prominent coastal headland). Duff was one of those very tall broad men—well over 6 foot –who immediately crowd a room with their size and confidence then recede into the background with their quiet demeanor. He had a wildly unrestrained white beard and even in old age his eyes were a strong bright blue, set under a mass of thin pale curls hidden by an ever-present navy toque. Loyal and kind to his dying day, he became my surrogate grandfather after Mum's dad died decades ago. He'd been a rock in my life ever since, especially so after I left childhood and craved adult guidance from someone who wasn't a parent.

The story he tells on these pages is one I'd never heard before. He'd kept it to himself but for some reason it began to eat away at him soon after he entered the Sydney care home. He became very moody during our visits and he'd lost some of the weight he'd put on over the last few years. I was only allowed to come once a month and could stay for only one hour, regulations put in place in 2022 after the horrific care home deaths in 2020. I thought it was criminal but what could I do? After snapping at me three times in the first five minutes of our visit, I confronted him. He told me, rather reluctantly, that he felt he couldn't die without telling this story. He didn't know how he could do it during our visits, when half the time was spent catching up on family news—and besides, he wasn't sure he wanted to tell it to *me* at all. They wouldn't let him talk to anyone else at the home for any length of time, either.

So we came up with a plan for him to record the story and me to transcribe it after his death. This is the result.

The only conflict I had with my promise to tell the story true to Duff's word was his tendency to use imperial measures like feet and miles when talking about the land but switching to metric measures like metres and kilometres when referring to the sea. A small thing you might say but I found all the back and forth a bit jarring. It makes perfect sense, of course, because Duff was taught imperial measures as a child but had to use the language of Canadian nautical charts once he went to sea in his teens. So I made an editorial decision to use metric only. However, for the sake of foot-pound readers, here are some *approximate* conversions for measurements that appear in the text that should get you by: 1 metre = 3 feet; 3 metres = 10 feet; 6 metres = 20 feet; 10 metres = 33 feet; 12 metres = 40 feet; 18 metres = 60 feet; 30 metres = 100 feet.

Duff's tale takes place in northern Cape Breton in Eastern Canada but more broadly within the Gulf of St. Lawrence, that enormous funnel-shaped body of water that connects the mighty Great Lakes to the Atlantic Ocean on the east coast of North America. The Gulf is unique for such a well-travelled region because parts of it become so covered in thick sea ice most winters that vessels often require icebreaker support between late February and May. The Gulf is also one of only a few places in North America with such a rich European and African history going back hundreds of years. My own family, for example, was originally from Africa, but came to the coal mines of Nova Scotia after more than a century in Barbados. Duff's family came from Scotland centuries ago, as did many in Cape Breton.

Duff's story has a lot of place names that will be unfamiliar to many readers, so I've included a map to help visualize the landscape of the Gulf. Here you'll find Neil's Harbour and Sydney on Cape Breton Island. He often mentions 'The Maggies', which you'll find called the Magdalen Islands near the middle of the Gulf on these maps, with the town of Old Harry marked.

I hope you have as much fun reading the story as I enjoyed putting it down for Duff.

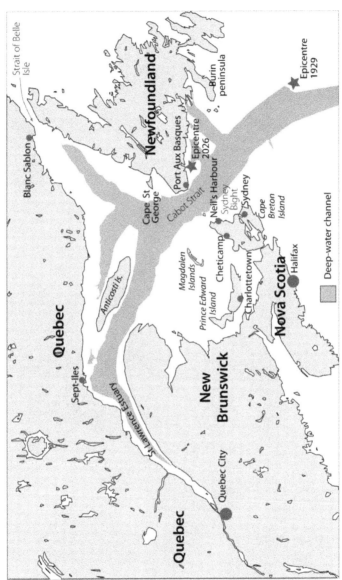

Gulf of St. Lawrence, showing marine channels
greater than 200m in depth.

Chapter 1

Duff's Preface, 2046

My name is Duffin Angus Gillies and I'm dying. Not today but soon. I'm ready to go. I'm old and sick but before I die I want to tell the story of something that happened back in 2026. I know some of it made the news at the time and scientific reports have been written about it. But for a Cape Bretoner like me who thought he'd seen almost everything, it was an experience like nothing I'd ever imagined. No one else around at the time saw the things I did. Not in my wildest dreams did I ever think I'd see the world turned belly up by a tsunami, let alone that polar bears would be part of it.

I was just the other side of 65 at the time, old already according to some. But I was still working the seals in the spring and making enough extra cash to turn the pension the government sent me into livable earnings. I wasn't fast but by God, I knew my stuff—not just the sealing, but the selling after. You had to work as hard to sell the catch as you did to land it in those days, even harder some years. I sold it all—the skins, the meat, the oil, even the teeth and whiskers.

I used to fish as well, as most sealers did, but gradually cut it back after I hit my late 50s and then quit altogether when the pension came in. Fishing is hellish hard work for months on end; sealing is challenging work for a few days. Sealing was always a bit of a lark for me, to tell the truth. Being on the ice was exhilarating if you knew what you were doing, deadly if you didn't.

That's why the kid came 'round asking me to teach her. If it hadn't been for her, none of this would have come out quite the same.

I'm trying not to ramble but I'm still getting used to this way of telling. There's nothing else to do anymore, really, at my age—and nothing else interests me except telling this story. So I'll just have to get on with it, as Nick said to do, however strange it feels to be talking to a machine rather than to a person. They won't let anyone sit with me long enough to tell them in person. For my own protection, they say!

It's a story I've never told before. Maybe because it seemed too terrible to admit I'd remembered every detail, like one of those crazy dreams you have you don't share with anyone because of what it says about you, that your mind would make up stuff like that. I think mostly I was afraid no one would believe me. But it's all I can think about these days: the year the polar bears came down out of Labrador and what they did in those few days after the ice tsunami hit. Everyone else remembers the sea ice rising up and the destruction it caused. I remember the polar bears.

Chapter 2

It all started on that trip I made north to the Maggies near the end of January. I had gone up to see Jimmy Bates in Old Harry. Jimmy is a sealer like me and we worked the seals together north of the Maggies the years the ice was light in the Gulf. But I hadn't seen him in four years, with the ice being so heavy, and he still had the rifle I'd left on his boat the last time we went out.

I guess that tells you how much I used my rifle. I hardly ever remembered I had it on the boat most of the time and now can't recall exactly why it ended up on the *Little Mermaid* in the first place. But there was an incident at the dock at Neil's Harbour before Christmas with some shifty, late-season tourists that made me realize I didn't have it onboard the *Ice Queen*—which made me remember I'd last had it on Jimmy's boat. The rifle came to mind again towards the end of January, after I got back from spending Christmas in Newfoundland with my good friend John Oliver—Nick's granddad—who'd been my neighbour in Dingwall years ago, as I got down to putting my gear in order for the sealing season. I decided I should really get the gun back from Jimmy before I headed out to the ice in March. I figured I had time to make a quick trip north if I left right away. There was generally only light ice around the Maggies before the end of January, even during the last few years when there'd been so much later in the month. The *Ice Queen* could handle most winter conditions but early-season ice meant I could travel faster.

So I got Jimmy on the radio and told him to expect me in a few days.

"Great timing, old man," he replied. "I've got a big surprise waiting for you."

"That's just what I need, Jimmy-boy. More surprises in my life."

He laughed at that and signed off.

I had a bit of work to do to get ready for the trip, mostly laundry and food shopping. I locked up the boat and headed up the dock on my way home.

I'd been there ten years by that point and Neil's Harbour had felt like home soon after I arrived. It was an easy place to get comfortable and not just because the people were friendly. The town was located at the eastern entrance to Highlands National Park, which attracted thousands of tourists every year. So many tourists passing through required a certain level of shopping and other amenities to keep them fed, healthy, and happy, including a hospital. And while those features put Neil's Harbour and its nearest-neighbour-community of New Haven in a good position to collect tourist dollars, they also made it a convenient place to live for locals.

The most memorable feature of Neil's Harbour was Neil Head, a substantial nature-formed spit that stuck out from the shoreline on the north side of town. The part connecting the spit to the shore was narrow but quickly widened out to twice the size of a playing field. There was a road nearly up to the old lighthouse and the broad spit created a natural harbour to the south. A long breakwater of rock rubble, built decades before I arrived, curved south from the end of the spit and provided even more protection for boats tied at the docks. At the end of the spit stood the well-maintained lighthouse, which marked our biggest navigational hazard—Murdoch's Rock.

The lighthouse was a lovely old thing, as squat and square as the day it was built more than a hundred years before. The light itself had been automated long before I got there but still worked and was a point of pride for the community at a time when working lighthouses almost everywhere had been abandoned. The lighthouse itself was a useful landmark coming into the dock, even in daylight, but was also a beacon for the Chowder House, the town's only restaurant and bar that had been built in behind it on Lighthouse Road. That could be handy at times, made it a good meeting place.

On the other side of the Lighthouse Road from the harbour—that is, to the north of the Neil Head spit, was a little scalloped beach called Back Cove. North of this rocky beach was Shoal Point and beyond that, New Haven Cove, where the fish plant sat. The lighthouse, the spit and Shoal Point sort of belonged to Neil's Harbour while the base of the breakwater at New Haven Cove sort of marked the start of the town of New Haven—but in reality the two were only a few kilometres apart and functioned most of the time as a single unit. In fact, the road that ran from the Highlands Park junction north to New Haven was called the New Haven road even though it was the main road along the waterfront through Neil's Harbour.

The docks at Neil's Harbour took up less than half of the available space in the protected harbour. Beyond them to the south was a shore launch for small boats and a few commercial outfits. There were fifteen working vessels at the dock in 2026 and all but two were lobster boats. That made me a bit of an odd man out among the lobstermen, but they treated me OK. Neil's Harbour had been a good sealing base for me—I could get around to the Maggies easy enough if I had to when the ice was light, as it had been for most of the first few years I'd been there. And the fact that Neil's still had a working light was a huge bonus for a commercial boat like the *Ice Queen*—you only had to return a few times in the dark or fog to feel that sense of welcome and relief. That feeling of 'safe haven' kind of permeated the whole community.

[Is this rambling? Damned if I know. Nick said to try and describe places as best I could, to give folks a feel for where things were and how it felt to me. If that seems like rambling, I don't know any way around it.]

Where was I? Ah, yes—I was leaving the boat. I found my old blue truck where I'd left it in the parking lot across from Lighthouse Road. It started up but as usual took a few tries before it agreed to run. I headed up the spit towards shore and turned south onto the New Haven Road. It was only a short few blocks along the coast road to Oceanview, which ran straight back from the shoreline to the tree-line. My place was a couple of blocks shy of the end of the road. I'd come to like being so far back of the harbour, even if it meant I had to drive all the time. Truth was, it was the only place I could afford.

Until I bought the place, I'd worked out of a little cabin in Dingwall at far north end of the Highlands. But Dingwall got to be a mean place as I got older, especially in winter. Neil's Harbour was still North of Smokey but closer enough to Sydney I could get to the big city to connect with buyers for my seal bits. Easier as well to make the ferry over to Newfoundland to visit John in Corner Brook, without facing a winter drive over the Highlands. Even then, I couldn't have managed the move if my brother Billy hadn't left me his insurance when he died. Dead so quick from pneumonia he didn't even have time to tell his little brother he was sick. It wasn't much of an inheritance but enough for the little cottage back of the dock with a bit left over to fix up the boat.

As I pulled into the carport, I saw my neighbour Logan at my back door. Logan Wilkie was almost half my age but over the years had become a good friend. I always thought of Logan when I someone mentioned Vikings—fair haired, tall, and tanned, he had the features I imagined a Viking would have, including the broad shoulders. Since I'd moved to Neil's Harbour, we'd spent a lot of time together and he'd come to love being on the ice in winter almost as much as me. He'd even come out sealing with me a couple of times to lend a hand.

Logan ran a lobster boat, same as his older brother Pete and his father before him. He lived next door in a big house left to him when his parents died. The little cottage I lived in had been part of the Wilkie property. But Logan hardly needed as much space as there was in the big house, let alone an extra cottage. He'd rented it out for a few years but was happy to sell it off to me with a bit of land attached when I came around asking.

Logan was just turning to leave as drove in.

"What can I do for you, Logan?" I shouted as I slammed truck door closed.

"Hey, Duff. I was just coming to ask if you'd come with me up to Dingwall later this week to help me and Pete with his engine. I promised him when I was up at Christmas that I'd come back and help him out before the ice came in but I think we could really use your magic touch. Every time

11

the two of us work on that bastard of a motor it seems to take forever. But when you put your hands on it, the damn thing turns over like it's never given anyone any trouble at all."

"The problem is you two fools do nothing but tinker around at the edges of that engine, you show it no respect. It's no wonder you can't ever get it fixed. But I've got a better idea. I was just planning a quick trip over to the Maggies to get my rifle back from Jimmy. Why don't you come along and we'll do a stop-over at Dingwall? Once I've got you two set up wrangling Pete's engine into shape you can either wait for me to pick you up on my way back or catch a ride over the Highlands with someone heading south."

"That sounds perfect. When did you want to leave?"

"Tomorrow morning. I just stopped in to put some laundry on and then I'm over to the Co-op for groceries. I'll fill up with diesel after I get the food stowed onboard so we can get an early start."

"That's great, Duff. I'll let Pete know to expect us at the dock. Honk when you're set to go in the morning. I'll be ready."

***

12

I gave Logan a wave as I headed into the house. The washing machine was just inside the back door and my heavy winter boat gear was in a basket there ready to go. I threw it all in the tub with some detergent and got the machine started. Then I took my boots off and went into the kitchen to check what I called my 'boat store' to see what else I might need for this trip. Being on a tight budget meant I had to buy what I needed for the sealing season whenever it was on sale. So I always stocked up year round on non-perishables.

I'd converted the tiny second bedroom next to the equally tiny kitchen into a huge pantry. Doing that had been cheaper and more useful than making a bigger kitchen. I didn't do any fancy cooking anyway, so the single short piece of counter in the kitchen didn't bother me much but the shortage of cupboards would have driven me mad in short order. Storage was tight on the boat as well, so having almost unlimited space here at the house was a perfect solution.

I determined I had only a light shop of perishables to get—oranges, a cabbage, some carrots, cheese, eggs, and a bit of milk—so I set off for the store in New Haven, which took me back down Oceanview and then north a bit along the New Haven Road to the Co-op grocery at the base of Shoal Point, which defined the next cove up the coast. I was able to grab what I needed fairly quickly, as the store was oddly quiet and I had only Sadie at the cash counter to chat with. However, after I stopped to talk to Colin Tucker in the parking lot on my way out, I decided to head further north up New Haven to check in on my friend Ed Hatcher, Colin's next door neighbour. Colin said Ed had been laid up with the flu the last few days and could do with some company.

As I headed out to Ed's place, I noticed that the parking lot of the Co-op fish plant on my right, on the south shore of New Haven Cove, was buzzing with activity. Ah, I thought: shift change— two dozen or so of the workers who prepared winter snow crab and lobster were trading places. The plant would be busier still in the spring and summer of course, as more lobster came in and fresh halibut arrived. It wasn't a huge employer but having at least some year round employment made a real difference to the town.

I found Ed a bit down after four days in bed without eating much. His kitchen was oddly tidy after so little activity. I made tea for us both, grabbing some milk and chocolate biscuits from my grocery bag in the truck.

"Why the hell didn't you tell me you were sick, you old fool," I scolded him. "I'd have brought you ginger ale and crackers. Here, have a biscuit with your tea, you need it."

As he ate and drank his tea, I told him about my planned trip to Old Harry with a stop in Dingwall and by the time I was done my story he seemed in better spirits. Colin's wife was bringing some supplies later so he'd have something to eat when he felt able to keep down something more substantial. I told him I'd check in when I got back.

I had to shake my head as I pulled out of the drive. Ed was only 70 but he'd gone downhill fast in the last year. A few months ago something had sapped half the energy and strength right out of him. His wife had died well before that but it was like it hadn't really hit him that she was gone and then it hammered him with a sledge. All at once, he'd been consumed by a grief that aged him twenty years overnight. It was truly astonishing. But Colin said he and Lizzie would keep a closer eye on him going forward, which was a relief. On top of this trip north tomorrow, I would be out sealing soon and wouldn't be able to make sure he was OK on a day-to-day basis.

I stopped back into the store to get more milk and chocolate biscuits on my way home.

***

We were off in the morning before first light. I'd always loved heading out to sea as the sun rose. The changes in light are so subtle and then all at once, they're spectacular. Logan and I shared the first hour without talking, each with our mug of coffee, just watching the sea unfold with the new day, taking it slow to save fuel. There was no ice off the coast yet, of course, but I imagined what the same trip might be like when I set off sealing in a few months, with the light flickering off the new ice as I left Neil's Harbour, then dodging the floating pans of ice as I travelled north and then west into the Gulf.

I couldn't ever stop in at Dingwall on my way sealing because it was always socked in with ice at that time of year, so this trip was a real treat. I realized I hadn't been to Dingwall by boat in at least four years, although I'd driven there often in my truck. I realized I was very much looking forward to the sight of that bizarre bit of coast we call Aspy Bay.

On the charts and from the height of the Cabot Trail Highway above it, the area looks for all the world like an enormous dinosaur stepped in the mud, right there beside the Cabot Strait, and left his

16

giant footprint. From the water as you go north, you pass one shallow, lagoon-like bay after another, four in all. Each is surrounded by low-lying land with some scrubby spruce, all but one with a sandy barrier spit across the mouth.

Two largest harbours flank the other two—North Harbour, where the town of Aspy Bay is located, and South Harbour at the other end. Those two are almost square they're so broad. Two short, narrow bays lie in the middle—Dingwall Harbour, next to North Harbour, is the smallest; Middle Harbour is a bit longer and sits on the other side of Dingwall. The town of Dingwall is located at the head of Dingwall Harbour, which is the only bay that lacks a natural barrier spit. The sandy spits of the other three all but seal them off from the sea except for a single narrow entrance apiece. Dingwall Harbour, not having a natural spit, has man-made breakwaters extending from each side to block the swell from Cabot Strait, leaving a deep channel in the middle open for boat traffic.

From the sea, these four lagoon-like bays are at odds with the rugged peaks of the Highlands in the distance, which look like a painted backdrop. North Harbour is bound on the north side by the hills of a fat finger of land leading to Cape North, the northern most point of land in Nova Scotia.

17

Well, that's not quite true—one long jump over the water from Cape North takes you to Saint Paul Island, which is truly the northern-most point. Aspy Bay's claim-to-fame is a spot just north of the spit across North Harbour where some say explorer John Cabot landed in 1497, which would have made him the first European to land on Canadian soil after the Viking intrusions centuries before. I don't know if that's true or not, but Cabot's Landing is a big tourist attraction that you can drive to from Aspy Bay. I've never bothered to go there myself.

As I steered the *Ice Queen* past White Point and headed northwest toward South Harbour, I asked Logan to take the wheel so I could fix breakfast. I went below and fried sausage rounds and scrambled eggs to put between toasted bagels for a quick meal we could eat in the wheelhouse.

"We'll want to get started on that motor as soon as we get in," I said, handing Logan a stuffed bagel in a paper towel.

"I expect Pete will already be at it, cursing the damn thing so that it's good and ready for you to treat it with respect," he replied with a grin.

"You'll be sorry one day, cheeky bugger. One day that engine will just give up completely and nothing I do will fix it. Pete's been lucky it hasn't quit while he's been at sea and out of reach of my 'magic' hands."

"He came damn close this time, from the sounds of it—limped back to port with it sputtering and coughing the whole way. Scared him silly, he said. A hold full of lobster he needed to cash in to get his boat payment in on time."

"He's going to have to spring for a new engine sooner or later, Logan. I hope he's putting some cash aside for that, or it'll hit him hard."

"Yeah, I told him that too. He does try, he said, to get a bit ahead with every trip out. But the longer he can keep this one going, the better the chance he'll have enough in the bank when it finally gives out. He'll still have to go for a rebuild, though—no way he'll ever afford a brand new one."

There wasn't anything more to say so I scanned the horizon towards shore. We were still running northwest and the shore was pretty featureless. But it was a clear day and I could see the Highlands in the distance. After awhile, I could just make out the low spit across the mouth of South Harbour, highlighted by the waves breaking against it. The winds were light but there was a bit of swell coming down the Strait. With luck we'd be at the Dingwall dock before noon, so I gave Pete a quick call on the radio to let him know we'd be in soon.

***

I called Logan up from below once we were off the spit across Middle Harbour. He came into the wheelhouse just as the Markland cotttages came into view on the hill above the sandy beach to our left. Closed up for the winter, of course, the resort sat on a high spot between Middle and Dingwall Harbours. Without even a dusting of snow on the ground, we could see the end of Dingwall Road leading up to the resort. Dingwall Road ran along the south side of the Dingwall harbour while Quarry Road fed the north side. The mouth of Dingwall Harbour was coming up fast on our left and the gap between the breakwaters was in sight. Without me having to ask, Logan headed to the stern of the boat to see to the lines. There was still plenty of time before we got to the dock but it was better not to rush.

As we passed through the breakwaters on either side of the entrance, some kid waved to us from an ATV parked at the end of the Quarry Road. I glance back to see Logan return the greeting and I gave the horn a little toot for good measure. As the commercial dock was only about a third of the way into the harbour, it only took us a few more minutes to reach the local boats.

Pete was standing at the stern of his boat, waiting for us to pull up, a huge grin on his face. Unlike Logan, Pete was far from Viking-like. He was dark haired and a good head shorter than Logan with skin twice as fair. Pete's face was reddened, as always, from the having the wind and sun on it day-in and day-out. His short beard and hair were more salt than pepper now, lighter than I remembered from the last time I'd seen him. I put the *Queen* in beside him, to make it easier to transfer any tools or parts I might need for the engine repair. Logan tied us off to Pete's cleats and jumped over to give his older brother a hug. I gave them half a minute then crossed over to the *Blue Betty* and said hello to Pete as I made my way to the engine room.

"Let's see what you've set me up against this time," I said as I passed. "I need to get over to the Maggies before the ice sets in, so let me get this damn thing apart so I know what parts we need to fix it. Then I can say my hello to folks."

I knew that wouldn't work, of course, but thought I might get halfway into the engine dismantle before I had to deal with my social obligations. I was wrong.

21

It wasn't ten minutes before heard Rory McInnis come aboard, deep in the middle of a story he was telling Pete in that loud, distinctive voice of his. After a few minutes, I heard footsteps overhead and a shout as he stuck his head down the forward stairwell.

"Duff! You coming up to say hello or what?"

"Give me half a minute, Rory, I'll be right up," I shouted back, knowing full well the man had no sense of time and that I may have bought myself at least another 15 minutes. I figured that was enough time to get done what I needed to do if I worked quickly. I gave up when I felt another two bodies come aboard.

I headed up the stairs, wiping the grease off my hands. As I poked my head up, I saw Neil Gallant and Tommy Martell had joined the party. Neil was a friend of mine from way back who still ran his boat out of Dingwall and was now the only sealer in a dock of lobstermen. Tommy was Pete's mate and had fished for lobster out of Dingwall as long as I'd been sealing. Tommy looked more like Pete's brother than Logan did, they were so similar in size, colouring, and temperament it was no wonder they got along so well. I shook my head in resignation and turned to Pete.

22

"You'd better put the coffee on. Before long we'll have Benji here with his mum's cake and we'll need something to wash it down."

Pete laughed and went below while I settled in for a visit with my Dingwall buddies. I wasn't really put out, it was good to see them all. And by the time the coffee was ready, Billy Young and old Sam Forbes had joined us, eager no doubt for the rum that Pete would provide to cool down the coffee. And before we'd all got our coffee poured, Benji showed up as predicted with a walnut coffee cake his mum had just delivered. As good a lunch as any I'd had and most welcome.

After several hours, Sam and I got to talking about engine troubles, which Sam always had aplenty. I expressed my preliminary diagnosis on Pete's diesel engine, which got argued around for a while. When I pulled out the broken part that had led me to my conclusion, they all went quiet. Pete broke the ice.

"Well, that settles it, I guess. But I won't be able to get a new one for at least two days. It'll have to come in from Sydney."

"I'll head over to the Maggies in the morning," I told him. "Now that you know what it is, you and Logan should be able to get the part installed when it comes in and get the engine back

23

together. I can stop in on my way home to make sure you've got it right, then take Logan back with me."

"That suits me fine," said Logan. "Let's get the parts order in before it gets too late, then we can all relax."

So we moved the party to Neil's house a few kilometres down the Quarry Road and had a good visit. Pete's little shack of a cabin in the woods behind the dock wouldn't have been nearly big enough for this gathering—he only lived there because he didn't like being far from his lobster boat and that was the only available land within walking distance. A steady stream of visitors came by to say hello once word got around I was in town. Someone brought a thick moose stew for supper and a big box of raisin cookies. Another added a pot of chowder and biscuits; bottles of rum appeared without a word. Mugs, bowls and spoons were all that was needed for this feast and many had brought their own in anticipation.

I took myself off back to the boat as early as was polite, since I needed to be up again before dawn. I shortly fell into the deep, contented sleep that comes when you know you're surrounded by friends.

***

I was up and heading out to sea, all alone, before first light. It was still dark as I passed across the mouth of North Harbour and Cabot's Landing somewhere beyond on the port side.

It was about a six or seven hour trip to the Maggies from Dingwall against the current and the day was shaping up to be as fair as the day before. I made up some sandwiches before I left and had coffee in a thermos to keep me going. There wasn't usually much marine traffic along the route I was taking but you still had to stay alert. As usual, I kept my eye out for large and small whales among the drift logs in the low swell, even though it was late in the season for them. It was a long but pleasant trip.

As I finally got the docks of Old Harry in my sights, I wondered for the first time since setting out what Jimmy had up his sleeve. He could be a bit of a jokester when he got an idea of playing fun in his head but it seemed odd he needed me in Old Harry for this trick to work. He could hardly have expected me to come for a visit at this time of year.

Old Harry is in the northern part of the Maggies on the island of Grosse Île. The long beach beside Old Harry was once a regular haulout for thousands of walruses, but the Basque slaughter of the animals for oil in the 17th and 18th centuries wiped them all out. Grosse Île now has a working salt mine that seems quite profitable but is otherwise an island of fishermen. And although the Maggies are governed by French-speaking Quebec, Grosse Île is a bit of a haven for English-speakers. It's one of the reasons my friend Jimmy chose to stay there. Jimmy settled in Old Harry after he first went to sea because he loved the Maggies but had never learned to speak French. Since I hadn't either, it was my favourite spot on the islands as well.

I slowed right down and pulled deep into the harbour where Jimmy kept the *Little Mermaid*. You could spot his damn boat a mile away with its bright pink trim. Jimmy had never been afraid to let his odd sense of humour show.

I cut the engines and let the *Queen* drift in gently alongside the *Mermaid* as I gave a brief wave to Jimmy standing ready at the midship cleat. Jimmy was almost as tall as me but strong enough to still be fishing, despite being several years older. He'd been a real redhead in his youth but the colour seemed to have washed out of him by the time he hit 60—his long hair and beard were now pale blonde riddled with white and his bright blue eyes had faded to ice. But there was nothing cold about his personality. He loved everyone.

When he tied the line, I ran down to throw the fenders over and help him tie the bow and stern lines. As I stepped over the side to say hello, I noticed someone else had joined Jimmy on deck—a rather tall young woman in working gear, with a dirt-smudged pale blue toque on her head. Jimmy was grinning like a fool.

"Duff, meet Izzy Walker. She'd like you to teach her how to hunt seals."

I just stood there. To say this was a surprise was an understatement. Never in my wildest dreams had I expected something like this. I simply didn't know what to say.

"Izzy came here looking for someone to take her sealing." Jimmy added quickly. "I was just going to send her over to Neil's Harbour to find you when you called to say you were coming. I said you were the best teacher around and if she wanted to learn to hunt, she'd do no better than to go to the ice with Duff Gillies."

"I figured she could go back with you tomorrow," he added.

I just looked at Jimmy. He must have gone completely mad.

"Don't look at me like that, Duff. I've spent a bit of time with her—put her to work helping me get the boat ready to go out. She's a strong, sensible girl. I think she'll do OK. And she says she'll pay for gas."

I looked back and forth between the two of them for a bit then extended my hand to Izzy. She had a firm grip and rough hands. Jimmy broke the silence again.

"Duff, why don't you walk up to Annie's and say hello, stretch your legs a bit? Izzy and I will put some supper together. Izzy can answer your questions while we eat, give you two a chance to get acquainted, before you decide."

I looked Izzy over again, then back at Jimmy, before I responded.

"OK, you win. I'll be back in an hour or so."

***

I eventually got why Izzy wanted to learn to hunt seal, although I didn't at first. She said she was a city girl from a Newfoundland family displaced to Halifax. She was 26 years old. With her toque and jacket off, sitting at the table to eat, I could see she had long black hair fastened in a tight braid down her back. She was a head shorter than Jimmy—still tall for a girl—but lean and wiry. There was a Spanish look about her that was almost exotic in this land over-run with Scots and Irishmen.

28

She said she'd studied biology at the university and learned about the harps: how the pregnant females come down from the Arctic to the gulf to give birth to their pups, nurse them for a short two weeks and then leave them on the ice to fend for themselves as they go off to mate with the dogs.

"But I need to know the world the harp seals live in, what it's really like to be on the ice," she told me earnestly. "And how a modern hunter fits into that."

She said she knew that for decades the newly-weaned whitecoats were the focus of the seal hunt but that that sort of killing had ended in the 1980s. I told her I'd lived through the transition from whitecoats to beaters and was all for it.

"I think beater skins are nicer, to tell the truth: bright silver-grey with black spots, all new-grown hair. Young beaters are not that much bigger than whitecoats—they're only a few weeks older, after all—so they're almost as easy to handle. It was never the killing I enjoyed anyway but the thrill of being on the ice."

"Yes, I can see that," she said eagerly. "My granddad felt the same about hunting caribou in Newfoundland. Said he just liked being out in the woods and seeing if he could track one down—

getting meat to take home for the winter was a bonus."

I explained that taking beaters took more skill than whitecoats because the ice was even more unpredictable late in the season.

"Some years the ice is unbelievably thick because of the wind and cold, and in others the pans are so thin and patchy it's like walking on water. You need ice sense in your feet to hunt beaters and that takes time and experience to learn."

"I'd really like to try," she said earnestly. "I'm pretty quick on my feet. I'd like to learn as much about being on the ice as I do about the hunt. I really wish you would give me a chance, Duff. It's not so much the killing I'm after but the stalk on the ice I want to learn. To understand what a hunter has to give in exchange for those lost lives. My mum loved seal flipper and while I don't relish it myself I do fancy sealskin boots. I think it's only fair and right to understand what's needed to have those things. I've saved two thousand dollars to put toward gas for the boat and food—if you'll have me."

Her attitude convinced me she might do alright.

I took another long look at her.

30

"OK, I'll take you on. I won't pretend that having you pay your way isn't swaying my mind. But the ice this year is shaping up to be about the same as the last few, so it should provide good conditions for learning what you need to know. We'll leave tomorrow for Neil's Harbour but I can't say when we'll come back in—it all depends on the ice."

"Deal," she said with a grin. It was the first time I'd seen her smile.

***

I had to move some gear out of the way in the small stern cabin and shift my own stuff back there so that Izzy could have the forward bunk next to the head. I explained about using the marine toilet, which was a finicky bastard at the best of times. She didn't blush or flinch, even asked what to do if it backed up despite best efforts.

We left before dawn the next morning. Izzy was down pulling in the lines and I was just about to put the boat in gear when I remembered why I'd come.

"Damn it!" I shouted. I threw the engine into neutral and ran to the door.

"Izzy! Hop over and get my rifle from Jimmy. I think he said he'd put it in the wheelhouse."

She quickly retied a midship line and stepped back onto the *Mermaid*. Moving like a cat, she disappeared into the wheelhouse. A few seconds she later popped out with a rifle case held high, making a questioning gesture with her other hand. I gave her a thumbs-up, so she scampered back towards the *Queen*. She paused for a second before she stepped aboard and looked behind her. When she turned back again I could see she was grinning. She hopped aboard with the rifle and set us free.

As we moved slowly through the main harbour channel towards the sea, I watched her coiling the fore and aft lines, putting them carefully back in place. A moment later she slipped into the wheelhouse with the rifle in her hand and without a word set it in the back corner.

"What was so funny?" I said to her back when she was already out the door. She turned around and came back to the doorway.

"I thought I'd managed to get clear without waking him," she said, leaning her head in. "But as I went past the door to the forward cabin I heard

Jimmy yell that you'd forget your damn head if it wasn't attached."

I laughed out loud at that. "True enough, though, and getting worse every year."

She went below for coffee but took it out on the stern bench to drink. I let her be.

When I looked back a while later she was gone and soon there were food smells coming out of the galley. Izzy appeared again at the wheelhouse door with two grilled cheese and sausage sandwiches wrapped in paper towel. She handed me one as she took a bite out of the other.

"I figured I should get to know my way around. That stove gets very hot."

"Yeah, it's handy when you need boiling water in a hurry but hard to control when you need low heat. Best to start as low as possible and go up from there."

"So I found out. Almost burned these."

"Mine's OK, I like them crispy."

We ate in silence after that, Izzy gazing out over the water from the other bridge chair.

When I had finished eating, she spoke up.

"How long will it take to get to Dingwall?"

"From here? A few hours."

"Can I see the chart? I'd like to get myself oriented."

I pointed to the marine map behind her on the chart table, so she swung around and hopped off the chair for a closer look. She spent the next half hour or so looking over the chart before she got back onto the chair and settled herself in. She looked oddly content.

***

We chugged through the breakwaters at Dingwall just after noon—the current going our way had helped us make better time than I had managed going out.

I explained that we really only had to give Pete's engine a quick check to make sure it was running properly, and if there were no problems we could continue on home and make Neil's Harbour before dark.

I think I'd forgotten to mention Logan coming back with us, but I couldn't see why that would matter. We heard Pete and Logan on the *Blue Betty* before we saw them, curses and loud voices spoiling the quiet of the mid-day dock. They must have felt the bump as we came alongside, as Pete's head soon popped up from below. As Izzy worked at tying up the *Queen* to Pete's boat, as she had seen me do at Old Harry with Jimmy's boat, Pete fairly exploded.

"Damn it, Duff! I still can't get the damn thing to run smooth. It goes, but it just doesn't sound as it should."

"Alright, alright! Settle down. Get out of the way and let me have a look. Pour young Izzy here a cup of coffee, she'll be needing it. She's going with me to the ice this season to learn to hunt. Don't you give her any trouble, she's a paying student."

Pete gave me an odd look but shrugged and headed for the galley. I went below and found Logan quietly cursing the diesel engine. I motioned him out of the way and asked what the trouble was. His rather jumbled explanation sounded like not enough air intake to me, so I checked and found the air filter needed replacing. They had probably been looking for something more complicated. Luckily Pete had a replacement in his tool kit, so I switched them out and started it up again. Purred like a kitten.

As I wiped my hands, I looked up and saw Logan watching Pete and Izzy talking on deck.

"Who'd you bring with you, Duff?"

When I explained why she was there he snorted his derision.

"You're going to take a girl to the ice?" he said in a low voice, his face turned my way so she wouldn't hear. "Why would you do that? Doesn't make much sense to make your life more complicated than it needs to be."

"Actually, it makes perfect sense for me. I think it will be fun. Sealing is different from lobster fishing, Logan. It takes finesse. Izzy wants to learn and I don't mind teaching her. Someone who already knows the hunt is about more than killing things is someone worth spending time on. Don't you give her a hard time—she's a guest on my boat same as you. She'll pull her weight. I have a feeling she's going to do just fine. Now go and get your gear—I want to get going right away so we can be home before dark."

Logan sighed heavily and shook his head, then shrugged and headed up top. I put away the tools he and Pete had left scattered around the engine room then followed him onto the deck.

"That should do it," I said to Pete. "I think she's ready for one more run at least."

"Thanks for stopping back in Duff, I appreciate it. I may only have time for one more run before the ice sets in. I'll be very glad not to miss it."

"Not a problem, Pete. But we really should be on our way. I'm on a mission now and need to

36

get the boat ready for some ice hunting before the seals come in."

Even Izzy raised an eyebrow at that, so I explained.

"You can't really learn about ice until you see how it develops in different situations. We need to find some young ice that's growing slow enough you can see how that happens. We need to get out in the Gulf as soon as possible."

Chapter 3

Logan stayed up in the wheelhouse with me as we left the dock. Izzy, perhaps sensing his antagonism, headed below as soon as she'd stowed the lines. Suited me fine for now but I figured he'd come around eventually. Fishermen were a stubborn, suspicious lot at the best of times and even in the twenty-first century many were oddly superstitious about having a woman on board even if they would never admit it—especially the young ones like Logan.

Izzy and I set out a few days later, early February by that time. The *Queen* was stocked with enough food and gear for a three week trip. A tight fit to get everything in—I had to use every nook and cranny on the boat. I hadn't been out for that length of time in years. We travelled all around the western part of the Gulf, out in the new ice so she could see it grow. Close to shore, off shore, out in the channels. Understanding the ice meant learning how it changed from frazil crystals to slushy slob ice flexing over the water like thick crude oil, to lovely level pans that thickened in place. Those level pans could get turned by the wind into jagged fields of concrete-hard ice thicker than the height of the boat but we wouldn't see those until later in the season.

She caught on quick how the ice differed in strength and texture according to its thickness, age, and history with wind. Even more so, the different sounds it made as the boat cut through and felt underfoot. Snow made all this more complicated. Thick snow over slob ice was the worst but she only got caught on that a few times, wet and dangerous lessons. You soon learn to *step* onto the ice rather than jumping off the boat because it gives you a chance to judge the feel of the ice—most times, you can tell if it's OK to put your weight down or not.

Ice sense in your feet is hard to learn; some kids just never get it. But Izzy picked it up quick. She learned to judge the ice from that first step, as quick as any young buck I'd ever been out with. Sure she got wet up to her armpits a few times but she learned. She said she'd done dancing when she was in school and maybe that helped her be light on her feet, even as big as she was. Boxing used to do that for the boys, I thought. Funny I never considered dance might do the same for girls. I never took a girl out to the ice before but then, none ever asked to go.

Izzy approached everything with a confidence I'd never seen before in someone so young. It gave her an air of fearlessness. But she was never reckless like some lads can be. She was just a fast learner and trusted her mind and body to do what was needed. If she really wasn't sure, she'd only look up at me with a raised eyebrow and if I didn't raise mine back, away she went. She was strong enough to work all day. And if she was cold she didn't whine, she went and got a sweater—or asked for mine, cheeky devil.

She wasn't the chatty sort—asked questions when she needed to but mostly watched and listened. I expect I over-answered many times, falling into a story or two about times past when it wasn't really needed. But she never showed any impatience with that, except the time her feet were getting wet as a result. She didn't say much about herself, although she did say comment once that her mum had got the idea for her name from the internet, which seemed to annoy her. Apparently, leading Egyptian goddess Isis had a son known as the "Gift of Isis" whose name was Isidore. Her

40

mum used the female form of the name, Isadora, for her only daughter. Izzy hated the formal name—said it sounded prissy—and had early on refused to respond to it until everyone called her the short version, even her mum.

Once, as I washed up the dishes after supper, I'd been telling her about the summer I spent working a coal mine before I was out of school, how awful it was to be off the water and she chipped in with a story of her own.

"I spent a summer with my auntie in Maine, the year my father lost his job. I think my parents wanted me out of the way for a bit since my dad was having a hard time of it. They didn't want me to see, I found out later. I was twelve years old that summer and I'd never been inland before. I'd lived beside the sea my entire life. It was so different. I didn't hate it. It had its own kind of beauty and quietness. But it really felt like another world. Alien, almost."

"That would pretty much describe a coal mine as well," I added. "Except it was really awful—ugly, dark, and dirty, all at once. I hated it and swore I'd never go back. Went to the ice sealing the first chance I got."

"I could see that," she said. Then she put the last of the mugs away and didn't say anything more.

Yeah, it was a bit different having a girl on the boat but not much. She was such a matter-of-fact and sensible kid that it hardly mattered what sex she was. On the ice one day, when I was explaining about the dogs hanging around the bitches and pups waiting for a chance to mate, she asked if I thought the dog seals could smell it when she had her monthlies. I was a bit stumped as I'd never thought about it but said I guessed her human smell overpowered it.

Anyway, after that first run into the Gulf in February, we came back for a few days bit to restock. Then we were off again, finding thicker and thicker ice. The more she picked up, the more I found myself heading further out to find more ice to test her on, avoiding the frost smoke over the water as much as we could—and when we couldn't, made it a lesson in how to do all the same things when you couldn't see for the fog. It was really cold out on the water by then and the ice kept getting thicker. Then the gentle weather turned and from then on we had one storm after another—buckled up the ice real good in places just when that was the next lesson Izzy needed. There were brief lulls of calm in between the storms, just enough to let the ice thicken up again. But we got out and walked the ice whenever it seemed safe enough.

Izzy'd chipped in for gas from her savings, as she'd promised, and I was having fun teaching, so there seemed no harm in the arrangement. Spoke to a fish cop beforehand to let him know what we were up to, swore on my mother's grave we wouldn't touch a seal until the official opening the third week in March. We were seeing quite a few around by that time. Izzy and I both enjoyed watching the bitches with their fluffy white newborns, some of them so fat they looked like fried sausages about to explode. It being so soon after the harp sickness at the Front last year—the one that caused the pups to be stillborn and had hundreds of polar bears coming ashore to hunt—I hadn't been sure there would be many harps around. But most of them seemed to have survived the epidemic just fine.

Thing was, it wasn't only ice and seals we saw. Just north of the Maggies past mid March we were out walking the ice and approaching a half dozen seals with pups hauled out a few pans over. It was still a bit too early to hunt. Most of the pups were whitecoats but a few were starting to turn into beaters, what we called the 'ragged jackets'– they

43

had that frazzled look baby birds get when start to get their flight feathers. Izzy was finding her footing on the wobbly pan she'd just stepped on, so her eyes were down. I saw it first. I said as low and calm as I could but still wanting to be sure she'd hear me, "Freeze. Ahead, 10 o'clock."

***

Her body stopped. Her head went up quick and turned to the left. She saw then what I did: a bloody big polar bear on a buckled-up pan just beyond the seals with his eyes locked on us. I'd never seen a polar bear in real life, let alone one down in the Gulf.

"What should I do?" she whispered.

"Just back up slowly. Keep your eyes on him and feel for a solid footing."

"But what if he comes at me?"

"Turn and run for the boat. I'll deal with him."

We both retreated backwards across that pan of ice then had to risk turning around to watch where we put our feet all the way to the boat, turning our heads back at every step to check he wasn't coming after us.

But after we had retreated a few pans, I realized his eyes had turned to the seals. Silly cows were totally unconcerned to have him so close, even with the wind blowing his scent their way. Odd, I thought—but wondered if that's why it's always been so easy to kill so many harps at once, down through history. They don't really scatter like you'd expect when you step on a pan or even when you walk around them. I guess I'd always thought it was only human hunters the bitches with pups were naïve about: it never occurred to me they would be so blasé with a natural predator of theirs almost on top of them.

Once we got aboard, Izzy was more excited and full of questions than I'd ever seen her.

"What the hell? What's a polar bear doing around here? I've never heard of one out on the Gulf ice!"

I told her what I could, which wasn't very much.

"You're right. We just don't get polar bears in the middle of the Gulf. I've never seen one before. But I heard stories a couple of years ago of a few bears on the Quebec shore west of Blanc Sablon, and one at the east end of Anticosti Island in the north Gulf. That was late in the season though and I never thought more about it. And there was a rumor of a bear off Cape St. George, on the west coast of Newfoundland last year but that just didn't seem plausible."

In truth, because of having Izzy with me, I hadn't been talking so much to the boys at the dock as usual and hadn't been as close to the radio as I'd usually been before the hunt. I wondered all of a sudden if I'd missed out on important word going around.

"What about this year?"

"I haven't heard anything so far. One guy last year said bears were coming down over the Labrador ice through Belle Isle to feed on carcasses of right and blue whales caught in the ice in the north Gulf. You know as well as I do, it's been a bad few years for whales jammed in the ice—we're getting more and more every year."

"Yes," she said. "That makes some sense, I guess. I didn't know polar bears would scavenge like that, though. There are definitely more whales around. The populations are finally growing after so many years of conservation. I've heard reports of whales trapped in the ice too but no one ever seems to explain why it happens. Is it just because there are so many more whales or are the ice conditions shifting, like everyone keeps saying—you know, because of climate change?"

"Nah, I don't think it's climate, it's got to be the sheer number of whales. We always did get low ice some years, even when I was first out as a boy. The season for sealing may be a bit shorter now than it used to be some years but there are so many more seals now than there were then that it doesn't make any difference to the total catch. We almost always get a few big storms with high winds every spring that rip some of the ice up real bad and pile it up against the shore. Some years Cabot Strait will get miles and miles of ice buckled against the Cape Breton coast—so thick even the icebreakers have trouble getting boats out. Even within the same year, the west coast of Newfoundland or north coast of Cape Breton will get totally jammed up from one storm and weeks later another storm will pile the ice up against the Quebec shore and through the Strait of Belle Isle."

"I could see whales getting caught in ice like that," I added. "I've heard some whales come through Cabot Strait from the south in February and March because they're heading to traditional feeding grounds of theirs along the Quebec shore. More whales overall means more coming though when there's still ice cover. They'd be safer to wait until after the ice clears, as most of them do, but maybe coming early has advantages despite the danger. Animals tend to do what's best for them, even if we don't always understand it."

As we talked, I got my binoculars out and looked back at where we'd seen the bear. It was then I realized there was a big hump of something dark in the pan of buckled ice he was on that could have been a whale. The bear was now beside it with his head down.

"Well, will you look at that?" I said with awe, handing Izzy the glasses.

"I wonder why he isn't going after the seals?" she asked, scanning the ice in front of us.

"He must prefer the whale lying there dead already, to the effort, however small, it would have taken to kill a seal or two," I told her.

I sure never expected to see a polar bear off the Maggies, I can tell you that. It made me wonder if I should be worried about the upcoming hunt. I now had my rifle back on board but had never taken it to the ice with me. Never saw the need. If you paid attention the way you should, even the aggressive dog harps are manageable with a gaff and nimble feet. When you're sealing you need a tool that helps you maneuver on the ice as well as for killing and a rifle just can't do that. I can't tell you how many times a gaff saved me from a death by freezing water.

I shook off the thought about bears on the ice, for the moment anyway. It was time to get serious and make a plan for the hunt. I decided we should head back to the dock to take on the last of our supplies before heading back out for seals.

On the trip back, after being very quiet for a long while, Izzy asked, "Do you think that was the only bear out there?"

That was Izzy for you: she often seemed to put my private thoughts into words. All I could do was shrug.

**

There was a lot to do once we got ashore and not much time to do it in. The hunt would open on Monday, March 23. That left us only a few days to get fitted up and out where we needed to be on opening day. Logan stopped over at the house while we were doing laundry and stayed for supper. He seemed much more relaxed around Izzy than he had been the day they met in Dingwall, even joked around with her a bit. It could have been because we weren't on the boat or the effect of the bit of rum he had in him, it was hard to say. But it certainly made for a much more pleasant evening than I had expected, given his previous attitude.

The next day, after sending Izzy aboard to stow canned goods and gear, I went in search of Captain Jake—little Jacob Sturgess that skippered the 60 foot *Bellie Mae*. He was the only other sealer on the dock, a squat, dark Scot who was also the worst gossip and biggest drinker. I never minded all that—having someone who knew what people were saying had its uses. I went to the Chowder House and saw him holding court in the back corner, half a dozen blokes hanging on his every word then erupting in roars of laughter. He got up for another and the lot at his table scattered into the room. I waylaid him at the taps and said I'd buy him a pint and chips if he had time for a chat.

He nodded and joked a bit with Angie at the counter as she filled the order, always the cheerful lass. We took our full mugs and plates back to his table, and I sat down across from him. After a few minutes of eating and drinking, he asked what was on my mind and I told him about seeing the bear.

His broad face crinkled all over with an ear-to-ear grin as he shook his head.

"Where the hell've you been, boy? There's been white bears sighted since early February, mostly in the north Gulf and off Newfoundland. Some boats out of Stephenville reported seeing bears along Cape St. George, all of them feeding on ice-trapped whale carcasses, sometimes several at once."

"But," he added, "so far as I know, no one's seen any around the Maggies. Where exactly did you see it? And why the hell didn't you put the word out on the radio?"

I told him where we'd been at the time and added, "I decided not to broadcast it because, to be honest, I wasn't sure anyone would believe me."

"It seems to be shaping up to be an odd year on the ice," he muttered, shaking his head. "After the carnage the bears caused over in Newfoundland last year, I'm beginning to think this year might be our turn. I heard a guy on the CBC, some Mountie wildlife expert—Luke something, I think—talking about the bear problems over there this year. There's been a few 'incidents' he called them, along the north shore and in Labrador, but nothing like last year. He wasn't very specific about whether anyone had been killed but said some bears had learned to come ashore looking for food last year so it was natural a few would be back again this year just to look around while they're waiting for harp pups to be born. Seal experts, he said, think the crop of pups this year will be back to normal at the Front—there should be lots of

51

natural food for the bears to eat and folks shouldn't be worried about them coming ashore like last year."

"Easy for them to say," I added. "You know as well as I do the papers only report what the experts want us to hear—they got that racket figured out pretty good. How would we know if bears are killing people if they decide not to tell us? I didn't hear anything when I was over at John's place over Christmas but that would have been too early, there wasn't enough ice then. Now that I think of it, I haven't heard from John since then. I'm sure he'd tell me if there was the kind of bear trouble that only locals would know about. But then, I haven't been around the house enough to bother checking my computer. Even when I have been there, it just hasn't been on my mind to check my email."

"Well, there's plenty enough ice now," said Jake, sounding impatient with my interruption. "The ice came in fast. The mountie said two whales got trapped in the Strait of Belle Isle when the ice piled up all of a sudden in early January and attracted dozens of bears, like flies on a dead rat. Now there's a few more whales trapped in the ice and lots for the bears to feed on. Started in the Strait, as the Mountie said, but then a few more carcasses near Blanc Sablon at the south end of the Strait pulled the bears down into the Gulf. Could be more whales along the Quebec shore west of there without anyone being the wiser, even some off the east end of Anticosti—plenty enough reason to keep the bears down in the Gulf until the seals whelp. Also explain how they got down to Cape St. George, which is a damn sight further south than I'd have imagined polar bears would ever go. You've been out, you know the weather's been awful—one storm, then another, wind from the south and then from the west, then back again. The ice is just a mess of buckled up ridges along the Quebec and Newfoundland coasts. Really, it's a wonder we're not socked in here as well."

"Has anyone been hurt?" I asked. "All those bears roaming around, you have to wonder."

"Not that I've heard. But who knows what will happen once the sealing starts and men are out walking the ice?"

He said again how surprised he was that I hadn't caught wind of it.

"The dock's been buzzing with talk of bears for weeks," he huffed.

I shrugged my shoulders in lame apology.

"Well, you know, I agreed to take this girl on as an apprentice for the season and it just took up more of my attention than I figured it would," I said quietly. "I haven't really spent much time at the dock over the last few weeks."

Jake just shook his head at my folly.

"Well, I'm out myself as soon as the season opens, heading to the North Gulf if I can get there," he said with good humour. "I'll keep in touch and let you know if any of those ice bears come to get me."

As I stood to go, I wished him luck and he nodded back the same to me. I left a half pint on the table, which I was sure he'd finish for me—but not until I was out the door, to be polite, as was his habit.

I pondered the news as I walked down the dock, wondering how much I should tell Izzy. I figured she'd earned the right to hear the truth, to not be coddled by withholding. I decided to tell her as we headed back out Sunday morning—all of it.

***

It was just before dawn and we were headed north out of Neil's Harbour in the *Ice Queen*. I broke my habit of silence over coffee—it just seemed the right time.

"What with the ice conditions and all," I said quietly to Izzy, "I'm going to head to the patch off the west coast and see how far south towards Prince Edward Island we can get."

She gave me a quizzical look but didn't argue. We were well underway and heading around the light at Cape North and on into Cabot Strait before she started talking.

"Why, of all the places open to us in the Gulf," she asked, "have you decided to go south? I'm not questioning your decision—I just want to understand the reasons. We didn't see many seals on our earlier trip to the east end of P.E.I."

"That's true," I admitted, "but often seals don't commit to a patch of ice until just before they whelp. We were there too early. And when I talked to Captain Jake, it sounded like there could be good ice down there right now for hunting. It's still within the official sealing area. But Jake said something else that made me think going south might be the best choice."

She looked at me with her head cocked to one side, again with that quizzical look.

So I told her about the bear sightings Jake had told me. She listened without interrupting until I finished.

"Do you really think it would be dangerous going back up to the Maggies? It sounds like you're not only sure there are more bears up that way but that we should avoid them at all costs."

"Well, the truth is I've heard some stories about what polar bears can do that will curl your hair. My friend John told me some of what really happened last year on the north coast of Newfoundland: the way the bears stalked and ambushed folks—then killed and ate them—sometimes breaking into folks' homes to do it."

"Only a few of those stories made the news, you know," I added. "But John talked to friends of his who'd lived through it and they told him how terrified they'd been to realize how defenseless they really were against a desperately hungry polar bear."

"The truth is," I admitted, "I don't like taking a rifle on the ice. But having one handy is the only way I'd feel safe walking the ice this year if we're north of P.E.I. We got lucky once: best not to press it. You might think I'm being overprotective but I'm protecting myself as much as you. I don't fancy being eaten alive, thank you very much."

"I really don't think a bear would ever make it as far as P.E.I.," I added, "so the south end of the Gulf should be safe. And if that means we get a few less seals than usual, I'm OK with that."

She shrugged and said, "Yeah, I'm OK with that too."

That was the end of it then, so we carried on.

***

We made our way to a patch about half way down the west coast and had good full day hunting opening day. I didn't want to go too far south and risk getting trapped. The ice off Inverness was just about perfect—thick enough for the seals but open enough for me to nose the boat through so we didn't have to walk too much.

On the second day, Izzy took a real dunking—went all the way under. She'd tipped a small pan jumping over a lead in the ice and had almost taken me with her. But I instinctively fell backwards to redistribute my weight, then rolled to the edge to fish her out with the gaff. Luckily, we weren't far from the boat and were able to get her into dry clothes and back out to the ice without losing much of the day.

"Not bad at all for a rookie to have only one full dunking this far," I said sincerely, as we sat over our supper that night.

"I was scared, I'll admit that," she answered. "But I knew you'd get me out, so I wasn't in a panic."

57

"Well, if you knew I'd get you out there was no need to be afraid at all, was there?" I asked.

She glanced up at me briefly then busied herself with her food. I didn't press it and we ate the rest of the meal in silence.

Early the next day we got a strong wind from the west and the ice started to tighten up, jamming up against the west shore of Cape Breton. I had to head north in a hurry to keep from getting the boat stuck fast. It took a good three hours of dodging fast-flowing ice and ramming through thickening pans of ice to keep moving. But once free of that peril, we got into a patch of seals near the north end, west of the light at St. Paul, and took in a decent haul of beaters over what was left of the day.

As it was so far north, I took the rifle out with me but we saw no bears.

That night over supper, Izzy glanced up at me with a serious look on her face.

"Have you ever had a boat go down in the ice, Duff?"

"What makes you ask that?"

"Just wondered. You just seem like you're not afraid of the ice at all and I wondered if that's because you'd never had cause."

"Oh, I've had plenty of cause but I figured out early on that you don't have to go through every experience yourself to learn from it. You watch other boats around you while you're out— you see a mistake someone else has made and figure out in your head what you might have done differently if it had been you. You listen carefully to the stories told later on the dock—a story of a boat going down can tell you plenty about how to get yourself out of the same kind of jam. None of this keeps you out of close calls but it can keep those close calls from being fatal. Mind you, you keep these thoughts about how to do things different to yourself—I also found out early that no sealer or captain likes to be told he handled things badly, even if he knows himself what he did wrong."

Izzy smiled at that. Then she nodded and went back to her food.

By early the next day, the wind changed again and was blowing hard from the northwest. The ice would be fast getting tight in Cabot Strait and I knew if we didn't head home immediately we might not make it in at all. A storm like that piles ice up hard against the north end of Cape Breton and fills the whole of Sydney Bight with ice so thick small boats like mine can be crushed to kindling. So there it was: the weather ended our hunt early, as it so often did.

On the way home, with me at the wheel and Izzy scanning the chart, I got to thinking that Izzy had really been a wonder through it all. She'd been as much help on the ice as Jimmy Bates had ever been. We'd almost hit our limit of seals despite getting caught short of time.

"It's been a real pleasure," I said to her while I kept my eye on the ice-filled waters. "You've been a good partner."

"Best time of my life Duff," she answered seriously. "You're a good teacher."

And when I glanced back at her I saw a smile of genuine pride.

I smiled myself, then leaned over and turned up the volume on the radio to check on the chatter.

While we were out this time, I'd kept much closer tabs on the radio chatter, listening closely for any mention of bears. While we were off P.E.I., Captain Jake reported seeing more than a dozen bears along the west coast of Newfoundland on his way north, with thick ice buckled against the shore and bears feeding on four big whales jammed in the ice. Not something he'd ever seen before, he said, but by the time he got to the north patch of seals off Quebec, he wasn't seeing any bears and wasn't worried about sending his boys to the ice. A few sightings north of the Maggies came from other captains and a rumour of one sighted off St. Paul Island that could have been a joke or someone imagining things in the fog. But no trouble reported except for one close call for a boy who'd gone off kilometres from his boat along the Newfoundland shore near the Strait of Belle Isle and surprised a bear feeding on a carcass of something. The bear charged at him a short distance but didn't come after him when he turned and ran. Lucky bugger, he was.

So, we passed St. Paul's light heading east and turned south for Neil's Harbour. I tried to put thoughts of polar bears out of my head. But just when we were almost home, in as close to shore as we dared—we got jammed. Thick buckled ice held us in tight. Three days we spent trapped, taking turns keeping watch, hoping for the wind to shift and drive the ice offshore. I wasn't deeply concerned but slept lightly when I slept at all. Izzy, bless her heart, slept like a baby. I often gave her an extra hour or two before I called her out to take the watch. She didn't complain very hard.

And then the world literally turned upside down.

Chapter 4

It was well after dawn on the Sunday, just after 9, and Izzy was on watch. I was just coming out of a fitful sleep, only vaguely aware that the low background noise of ice grinding and groaning—near constant over the last few days—had been replaced by something else. I was already on my feet when I heard Izzy shout my name.

"Duff!" was all she said, her voice rising in a mix of warning, fear, and awe.

The first thought that came to my head was 'bear over the transom'. I grabbed my rifle and scrambled as fast as I could up the ladder.

I looked immediately to the back of the boat but saw nothing that looked like a bear. I turned and saw Izzy up at the bow looking out over the ice. I fixed my eyes that direction as I made my way forward to stand beside her.

"What the hell...," I muttered under my breath.

There was a roar like continuous thunder coming from the pack ice that was getting louder by the second. In the early morning light, I could see the ice cracking and heaving as it broke apart in front of our eyes, massive slabs thrown every which way. It was as if a giant sea monster was swimming just under the ice and headed straight for us. I'd once heard a sound something like that come from the bow of an icebreaker but there were no ships in sight—and I didn't think I believed in sea monsters, giant or otherwise.

The roar was coming at us like a train, increasing in volume the closer it got. It was so deafening it was terrifying, I have to say. And whatever it was, it was clearly going to pass directly under us. I had no idea what that would do to the boat, jammed in like she was. There wasn't time to do much of anything so I yelled at Izzy to hold on. We both turned and grabbed for the rail that ran around the wheelhouse, hooking our arms around it. I didn't much care for having my back turned on the approaching menace but there was little else I could do.

The din of crushing and cracking ice surrounded us as what felt like a small wave lifted the boat and passed underneath. The noise was momentarily all-consuming, leaving no place in my brain for thought. But the wild swaying of the boat told me the jolt had broken us free. Izzy glanced at me real quick and I could tell she felt it too. The racket of crashing ice then receded as it had come, passing away from us on the other side of the boat. We watched in stunned silence as the once solid expanse of ice between the boat and shore turned to tumbling shards and blocks the size of houses as the monster continued on its path. However, I had to put that thought of a monster out of my head because it was obvious now, looking at it from the backside, that there was a wave running under the ice.

Luckily, the movement of the wave through the ice had left us in a small lead of open water. I hoped we were in no danger of going down but I wouldn't know for sure until I got below to see what damage had been done. As we both stood there dumfounded on the bow, the roar of the ice rolling away from us towards the coast, I wondered what it would do when it got there. I guessed we would find out soon enough.

***

I looked into Izzy's terrified eyes and open my arms to her. She sank onto my chest, shaking

64

and muttering something I couldn't hear as I held her tight for a minute.

When I could feel the quivering lessen, I said, "We're OK, but we need to check on the state of the boat."

"Yes, OK," she said, and turned to move away as I loosened my grip.

But before we could take a single step to head below, we heard more crashing in the pack and realized another wave was headed our way. We grabbed on again as the second wave came and went, ice blocks tumbling and crashing together all around us without quite the din of the first time but raising the boat higher as it passed below. This time we waited a few minutes longer before trying to move and sure enough, a third wave came and went, leaving the boat rocking in its wake.

After waiting another 10 minutes without another wave, we made our way off the bow and down below.

"I'll check for water," I said as Izzy plunked herself down on the bench, still looking a bit shaken.

A quick check in the bow and engine well told me there was only one small leak. We'd got lucky.

"We aren't in any immediate danger of sinking," I told her, "but if we don't get moving we'll be trapped again when these ice blocks freeze together. We have to get out of here."

We both moved up to the bridge and as I started up the engine, the radio erupted in chatter. Mostly of it was along the line of 'what the hell was that' from boats far away from where we were, but it was hard to pick out anything of much use.

Izzy turned suddenly and looked at me with her eyes wide open.

"I think I know what it was," she said with excitement, "I learned about this in geography. I think we've just had a tsunami pass under us."

"Not a rogue wave?" I offered. "I've seen one out here in the summer but never even heard of one in the winter. I guess I always assumed winter ice like this was too thick for a wave to push up from below."

"Rogue waves don't come in threes, a few minutes apart," Izzy insisted, "but tsunami waves do."

"A tsunami," I muttered, shaking my head. "I never thought it would ever happen again."

I was remembering, of course, the tsunami that had happened before I was born.

"When I was out as a youngster fishing for the first time, I heard some of the oldtimers talking about the tsunami that hit the south coast of Newfoundland in 1929," I told her.

"I heard about that one too, from my great grandmother Annie a few years ago," Izzy added. "Annie's mother Mary and the rest of the family lived in St. Lawrence on the south side of the Burin Peninsula, before Annie was born. They all survived but lost almost everything."

"As I recall," I said, "the tsunami struck on a Monday near the end of November, just after supper. A moonlit night, they said it was. Apparently, there'd been an earthquake south of Newfoundland, out on the Grand Banks. A fairly big one, if I remember correctly. The quake triggered a landslide in the Cabot Strait."

"Underwater landslides can generate really dangerous tsunamis, especially in areas where earthquakes are common," offered Izzy. "We learned that in geography class as well. There was one in Indonesia in 2004 that killed hundreds of thousands of people—there was a large earthquake several hours before the tsunami hit but the waves still took people by surprise. They showed us videos of it—huge waves rolling relentlessly onto the shore like they were never going to stop."

"Yes, I heard of that one too, other side of the world. But we were talking about the Burin, don't distract me. What I heard was that the tsunami in 1929 floated buildings off their foundations or just shattered them to bits. Boats were sunk, smashed up, or washed out to sea. All along the coast of the Burin, entire stores of dried cod were washed out to sea—a year's supply of food for dozens of communities, destroyed in a flash. There were no roads on the Burin in those days, of course, so the outposts could only be reached by boat. And as bad luck would have it, their telegraph had gone down the day before during a big storm and no one outside knew what had happened until the next boat came in three days later."

Izzy added the story she'd heard.

"Granny Annie said the water in St. Lawrence harbour came up at least 12 metres. Before the water came in like that, it ran out of the harbour almost completely and they didn't know what that meant. But it scared the hell out of everyone and then they saw this huge wave coming in, like nothing they'd ever seen before. They all ran for their lives. If there hadn't been a moon, they wouldn't have been able to see it coming.

"As it was, they had just enough time to get off the docks and up to higher ground. They were lucky that the shore rose fairly steep behind that harbour. But they lost everything except the house: their boat and wharf, supply of flour and molasses, the winter coal, and all of their dried fish. The family ended up leaving a few weeks later on one of the rescue boats that was sent, begged to be taken out. Mary's husband insisted they wouldn't survive the winter. Granny Annie thought they would have managed but in the end they were able settle in St. John's with the help from a local church."

"Sounds like a very smart move to get out when they could," I said. "I don't doubt life would have been a living hell if they had stayed. It sure was a hard life in those little Newfoundland outposts at the best of times, fishing just enough to live. They had some luck surviving the waves in the first place, that's for sure—lucky there was a moon and lucky folks were out and about on the docks where they could see the first wave come in. I heard they'd all felt the earthquake on the Burin hours before the waves—like folks did here on Cape Breton—but none of them thought that an earthquake might be followed by a tsunami."

"Why would they? Izzy pointed out. "We don't get tsunamis here on the East Coast—they're a west coast thing. That's why they have tsunami warning systems out there."

"Well, even if there had been some kind of a warning system here, I doubt it would have saved the folks of the Burin—not with their telegraph lines down," I pointed out. "Even if there had been warning enough to save those lives, it wouldn't have stopped the damage. As your granny said, I'd heard St. Lawrence had almost 12 metres of water up the harbour, which I still find bloody hard to imagine. But even in other places on the Burin, the waves were at least 6 metres above the normal tide. That's quite enough to devastate most of those outpost villages perched on the edge of the sea. I was surprised to hear only two dozen or so people drowned."

"Well, I'm surprised how many people my age never heard of it," said Izzy. "And as far as I know, we still don't have a tsunami warning system like they do in the Pacific. I guess the earthquake experts here really didn't think it would ever happen again."

Our fears were confirmed moments later when the radio chatter was replaced by a Coast Guard marine alert:

"Tsunami warning for all coasts southern Newfoundland and northern Cape Breton. Dangerous coastal flooding and powerful currents; move to higher ground or inland. Port of Burgeo registered wave of 10 metres at 08:10. Monitor this channel for instructions regarding rescue efforts. Very thick broken ice in Cabot Strait and strong northwest winds may hamper vessel travel. Vessels at sea should stay at sea. Vessels en route to Sydney Harbour hold offshore until further notice."

Izzy looked at me with both eyebrows raised, an "I told you so" expression if I ever saw one, but didn't say anything more.

I did wonder, however, if any of those earthquake experts had ever thought about a tsunami happening in Cabot Strait when it was covered in ice.

***

Now that we had a better sense of what was going on, Izzy and I were eager to get home. I got the boat turned around and headed to shore. I had no idea if we'd make it there before getting jammed in again but we had to try. It was slow going, bumping our way through leads in the jumbled ice blocks. It wasn't much more than five kilometres to Neil's Harbour by my calculations but it took us

71

almost two hours to go a bit more than half the distance. Then the ice grabbed hold of us again and I couldn't get the boat to budge no matter how much power I put to the diesel.

Then I heard the tell-tale sound of water pouring in down below. Our leak was worse.

I told Izzy we were going to have to walk the rest of the way in. We went below and she put together something for lunch, but I can't for the life of me remember what. I pulled out the bottle of rum and poured us each a decent measure in our mugs: she topped hers up with a slug of canned milk, which I thought vile but was how she liked it. She did the same with coffee.

By the time we'd finished eating, there was an inch of icy water covering the floor. I told Izzy to gather up her hunting gear. I moved around the cabin filling a backpack I rarely used with warm clothes, extra gloves, and a bit of food. I attached my rifle to one side using the outside straps. I handed her the smaller day pack she usually took on the ice and told her to fill it with as much water and dried food as she could fit. Don't forget your gaff, I reminded her. I strapped my own sealing gaff to the other side of my pack opposite the rifle and grabbed the longer fishing gaff that lay on its hooks above the bench.

As I held it in my hands, the thought occurred to me that I'd never see this boat again. It had been an extension of myself for more than 30 years but now it was doomed. Without a second thought, I returned to the wheelhouse and used the gaff to pry the *Ice Queen*'s brass name plaque from the dashboard. It wasn't the right tool for the job and ripped up the polished wood surface but that hardly mattered. I slipped the metal plate into an inside zippered pocket of my jacket.

The last thing I did before I left the boat was send out a mayday on the radio. I didn't expect a reply under the circumstances and didn't get one, but felt obliged to tell anyone who might have been listening that we had abandoned ship and were headed to shore, just in case we didn't make it.

Izzy was already off the boat and didn't hear my call. Just as well—I wasn't quite sure if it even mattered. After the Coast Guard tsunami warning—and having watched the mayhem in the ice as the waves made their way to the coast—the thought of what we might find when we got to shore sat like a stone in my stomach.

I figured we were only a couple kilometres or so from Neil's Harbour but it was the toughest walk over ice I'd ever had and that's saying something. More climb than a walk, to tell the truth, and it was very cold. The jumbled blocks of ice were by now mostly fused into place but a few rolled perilously as you tried to climb over them. We didn't have the best boots on for the job and had to pick our way slowly. I eventually learned to poke an ice block with the long fish gaff to test how solid it was set. That helped our speed some but Izzy still got her boot caught between two blocks when one rolled oddly and I had a devil of a time getting her loose. We were just bloody lucky it hadn't snowed since yesterday or we'd have had a near-impossible journey in front of us.

After a devilish hard climb over a particularly jammed up bit of ice, I looked up expecting to see more ice. But ahead I saw something dark buried in the ice.

The first thing that came to mind was a dead whale, which meant a polar bear might already be on it. I took off my pack and unstrapped the rifle. Izzy cocked an eyebrow at me for a second, then her eyes went wide as understanding sunk in.

***

We picked our way forward more slowly, the dark thing in the water coming and going from view as we climbed. We both kept looking behind and to the side every few seconds.

74

Eventually, enough of the dark body could be seen that it was obvious it was not a whale but the underside of a black-bottomed boat. My relief was short-lived as my thoughts went quickly from fear for my own safety to concern over whoever had been in that boat. I looked around again and shouted.

"Hello! Anyone here?"

There was no reply. We climbed as fast as we dared towards the wreckage, calling out every minute or so, then stopping to listen for any signs of life. As we were almost upon it, Izzy heard something.

"Over here, Duff!" she called out from her position to my right. "I think I heard someone moan."

We both hurried to the nearest end of the overturned boat and saw a man lying on the ice, the lower half of his body pinned under a huge block of ice that no mortal would ever budge. He was barely conscious when we reached him, opening his eyes after some minutes of encouragement only to close them again. He wasn't anyone I knew. When I asked his name I couldn't understand the muffled response, but it could have been Saul or maybe Paul. Then I asked if there was anyone else with him and his eyes popped open immediately.

"Mary!" he said, clear as day.

"Your wife? I asked quickly, looking around.

"Dau...," was all he managed to get out before he closed his eyes again.

"His daughter," said Izzy quietly. I nodded agreement. As we watched to see if he had anything more to say, he exhaled loudly then went limp. He was gone.

It looked like he had been thrown off the boat by one of the passing waves and had been laying there for hours, pinned by the ice block, slowly dying of hypothermia and crush injuries. There was nothing we could have done to save him.

"Let's see if we can find her," I said to Izzy. "You take this end and I'll take the other."

We each set off, calling for Mary. I realized it might be futile because the child might be trapped underneath the overturned boat. But I headed off anyway for what turned out to be the stern end of the broken lobster boat. There was wreckage strewn all over the ice, broken bits of wooden wheelhouse, electronics, and glass. I spotted a life ring with the name *Blazing Glory* printed in fancy script around the edge and picked it up. At least we knew what boat it was.

And then I found Mary—or what was left of her. It took my breath away. Like her dad, her torso was pinned under a block of ice. But the rest of her was nowhere to be seen.

I didn't call out to Izzy immediately but moved forward and to the left for a better look. I saw an arm about a metre away. It was sticking out from under another huge block of ice. Around the back side of that frozen boulder I spotted long blonde hair splayed out on the ice. I groaned as I saw that the head the hair belonged to had been pierced by a shard of wood. Broken up by the force of the tumbling ice, a long piece of transom had been driven through the poor girl's face like a spear.

I closed my eyes and called out to Izzy.

"Over here!"

As I listened to Izzy pick her way over the ice towards me, I realized I could have walked back to the other end of the boat and said I hadn't found her, that Mary must be dead inside the overturned hull. I gave my head a shake. It was a gruesome sight, for sure, but death was a reality of life, especially on the ice. Death wasn't something I had a right to shield Izzy from, even this one.

***

"Oh Duff," she said, turning away from the carnage, shaking her head. "Poor girl. She never had a chance."

There was a bit of a catch in her voice but she didn't break down. I didn't try to comfort her. Instead, I sat on a nearby ice block and pulled out my water bottle. Izzy sat down beside me.

"There isn't anything we can do for either of them now," I said between sips. "We can't even move the bodies. But at least we can report the boat down," I said, holding up the life ring.

She nodded silently when I suggested we keep going. We both stood up and put our bottles away. I strapped my rifle back onto my pack and tied the life ring to the top, then followed Izzy as she scrambled over the ice.

I kept looking ahead for the lighthouse. After all this time, I thought we should have been close enough to see it. But there was nothing, just endless ice. Izzy caught me looking.

"Where's the lighthouse?" she asked.

"Maybe we haven't gone as far as I thought," I replied.

After a half minute of gazing out over the ice, she said in a quiet voice, "Maybe it just isn't there anymore."

"True enough. We'll have to wait and see."

I was glad in a way she'd seen the obvious and wasn't afraid to say so. It meant her usual matter-of-factness was intact. I was glad I hadn't held back on her about Mary, she'd earned that. We both deserved as much straight talk with each other as we could muster in what lay ahead.

Within short order we hit another ridge of ice, the blocks all jammed together into a wall at least 3 metres tall. It took 10 minutes to get to the top, Izzy following me as I picked my way carefully up an awkward sort of path. I took a deep breath before I reached the top, not sure of what I would see on the other side. I was filled with excitement as well as dread. Neil's Harbour had to be on the other side—we surely were close enough to see it by now.

I knew my little town was low-lying and mostly flat at the shoreline: it sat only 3 metres or so above the short rocky beach, and even Murdoch's Rock out past the breakwater barely rose above that height. Would that have been enough to protect it? Had the breakwater that protected that little cove where we docked our boats been enough to keep the ice out? What had happened to the old wooden lighthouse, more than a hundred years old, and the Chowder House in behind it? Further north along the shore in New

Haven, were the waterfront fish plant and the co-op grocery store still standing?

As my head went over the edge, I caught sight of the low timbered hill beyond the harbour. But other than that, all I saw at first was ice. Izzy right below me and asked if I could see the lighthouse. But I couldn't answer. She struggled her way up beside me and looked out over the ice. "Gone," was all she said. It was a very quiet voice, even for her.

We quickened our pace as much as we dared going down the far side of the ice ridge. I didn't think we were far from where the shore should be but I couldn't really tell for sure. There was ice half way to the trees and along the shore from south to north as far as we could see. All the flat land that had once been homes where people lived, lawns where children played, and roads where cars had driven, was heaped with massive ice chunks. And the little crescent-shaped harbour that once had been home to a dozen or so working boats, mine included, was nowhere to be seen.

As I searched the horizon to orient myself on this bizarre icy landscape, Izzy gave a shout and pointed. And I saw it then—my little white house with the red metal roof, still standing near the top of Oceanview Drive, the main road in town that ran straight back to the trees from the shoreline. In normal times, New Haven Road snaked around the waterfront from the hospital at the south end of town to the fish processing plant at New Haven. I realized then that we were already on land, or more rightly, standing over it: we were just about where the car repair shop should have been. It used to sit near the beach on New Haven road, on the south side of the harbour past the commercial dock.

Slowly, we began to pick out other structures still standing on the landscape: Clara Inglis's big yellow house over by Cabot Trail road heading up to the Highlands and Jacques Masson's bright blue lodge nearby; over on the north side of Oceanview, Liam Longhurst's big red truck parked in the driveway of his white house, framed against the dark trees. Then I saw people moving around beyond the ice.

I just looked at her when Izzy asked what we should do.

"Let's go home," I said after a minute. It was all I could think of to do.

So she followed me as I picked my way over the ice headed for my house. Again, it was slow going. The ice blocks were even more wobbly here than they had been out over the water. It was more like walking over boulders from a rock slide, which made our route anything but a straight line. Finally we cleared the ice field and got our feet onto Oceanview Road. But then we saw the effects of the water that had brought the ice in with it. The homes just beyond the edge of the ice were flooded rather than crushed. A lot of things weren't quite where they should have been: cars and trucks on back lawns, sheds in odd places, a small boat on a trailer tangled up in a hedge, a snow machine on top of a pushed-over fence. But the houses were still standing. And since my own home was still a bit farther on, I allowed myself a little twinge of hope.

Chapter 5

Making our way further up Oceanside, we ran into my neighbours before we got to the house and heard them yelling long before that: the Fitzgeralds, Will and Jane Bishop and their four kids, Kelly Madden and his wife Dawn, James Tulley—and Logan. They converged on us, chattering like a flock of sparrows. Logan gave me a big hug and said he thought I was a goner. Dawn came to Izzy's side to make sure she was OK. Finally, I held up my hands for quiet and asked what time it was. Someone called out "3:05". I looked at Izzy and shook my head. It had only been hours but felt like days.

Then I asked if just one person could say what had happened. Logan looked around and stepped forward slightly. His voice was shaking, which wasn't like him at all.

"This morning—just after 9 or so, I think—I was just about ready to go cut some firewood when I heard a roar like nothing I'd ever heard. I put my coat and boots on real quick and went outside. The sound was louder out there and seemed to be getting closer. I could just make out a hump in the ice just beyond the breakwater. I saw people running up Oceanview away from the shore. The sound quickly became deafening. Suddenly, the offshore ice rose above the height of the breakwater in behind the lighthouse in Back Cove.

"I stood there and watched the lighthouse literally explode. The wave hurled ice at the mid-section and just blew the top section right off. Within seconds the Lighthouse Road was covered with water and churning ice. I still can't believe it. That wall of ice crushed the lighthouse and everything else on the point—sheds, homes, businesses, cars, the Chowder House—and then swept overland to fill the boat harbour from behind. Then it smashed across the south side of the harbour to the lagoon in behind, taking out the post office as it passed.

"Up at the top of Oceanview here, it was total chaos: everyone was running out of their homes screaming, kids were crying, and most of the dogs were bolting for the trees. I think most people down below were saved because of the noise: that God-awful racket was something you couldn't

84

ignore. It told them to run like hell. A few have said they heard a warning on the radio or the internet—but the warning came only a few minutes before the first wave hit. Then another wave came, bigger than the first with even more ice, just minutes after. And then another. Those waves pushed a wall of ice further and further onto the shore, crushing everything its path. Folks had had just enough time to get ahead of the first wave, and as they ran the sound of the ice crashing behind them was all the encouragement they needed to keep going up to the tree line. A while after the roaring died down, they turned and saw the sea water receding under the ice that had been carried onto the shore. The water left behind a towering wall of jammed-up ice with the mangled debris of their homes embedded at the front.

"We're assuming that the folks who didn't make it out of their homes or businesses near the waterfront when the first wave hit are either drowned or crushed to death, poor buggers. Some left a little too late or weren't able to outrun the first wave. No one has seen any of the Hawkins family, nor the Dowlings—except for Nick, who was out delivering papers. We're pretty sure John Hatcher didn't make it out of his garage down on New Haven—his wife said he'd gone in early to do some welding and figures he must not have heard the sound of the ice breaking until it was too late. Billy Budge hasn't been found but his beat-up old truck is jammed up in the ice wall over there.

We think that most of the folks who lived back of the shore but below Cyril's Drive made it out in time but their homes have either been smashed or flooded. Neighbours further up the road have taken in these folks for now—they want to be as far from the wall of ice debris as they can get. The high end of Oceanview, from about here on back, seems to have escaped the devastation from the waves, except for some flooding."

Logan looked to be clenching his teeth as he finished telling his story. I looked around and could see that one little cluster of homes, including my own, lay just beyond the destruction zone behind Cyril Road but had suffered some water damage from the run-up of the waves. My old blue truck was still under the carport where I'd left it, but had been rotated by the water and sat at right angles to the house.

As he saw me looking, Logan added that his house, because of the way it was built, had water damage to the basement but his new jeep had been untouched. But he had spent all day worried about what had happened to me and Izzy. His radio at the

86

house had gone out the day before, so he hadn't been able to reach me and now his radio-equipped lobster boat—filled with gear and provisions for the upcoming season—lay splintered beneath 3 metres of ice. He was really worried about his older brother Pete, who still lived up in Dingwall. Logan's voice cracked in a funny way as he said he hadn't been able to reach his brother. He hadn't seen him since we'd made that run up after Christmas and was now consumed with the thought he'd never see him again—he really looked shaken. But when Dawn reached over to put her hand on his arm to steady him, he shook it off and tightened his jaw again.

"An hour or so after the ice stopped coming in," he added, with some effort at calming himself. "Angus Gibbs up the road called the Buchanan Hospital. They said the road out in front is covered in ice and the building has some water damage on the ground floor but is otherwise OK. It's acting as a place of refuge for the survivors from that end of town whose homes have been destroyed. They said they had surprisingly few injuries among the survivors—some scrapes and bruises, and one broken leg."

Gesturing away to the north, Logan added that Angus had also talked with the chief of the volunteer fire department at neighbouring New Haven, which lay less than a few kilometres along the coast road. Because of the direction of the ice waves and the configuration of the New Haven harbour, the waterfront there had been hit hard. Logan pointed out what we all knew—there were dozens of homes in New Haven close to shore. However, all but two families had made it out alive. The few minutes warning had been just enough to save them.

The fish plant and its loading dock were completely destroyed, and a few employees on the early shift had perished, likely because the noise of the power washers had drowned out the noise of the approaching ice until it was too late. Folks who lived well back of the harbour at New Haven had survived with their homes intact, and that included one of the doctors from the Buchanan, who was able to treat the three people who'd been badly injured. There was no way to get any of them to the hospital, as most of the road along the shore was covered in ice.

Logan also said that someone at the Buchanan had contacted the Coast Guard and the Royal Canadian Mounted Police and given them a status report of the situation. The Neil's Harbour and New Haven survivors had been told they were on their own for the next few days, as many communities were in much more need of immediate help. They were told the damage from the tsunami had been wide-spread and devastating and that the city of Sydney had been particularly badly hit. By then, that wasn't really news, as a few people still had cell phone and internet connection and were getting early reports of what was going on in Sydney and elsewhere. It was bad all over.

As Logan finished his accounting, I looked around at all their faces. Logan looked spent. Kelly suddenly declared it was supper time, and ordered everyone to their place to eat. We could bring food if we had it but we should all eat together, despite the early hour. I really wanted a bath but didn't have the strength to argue. Logan declared he would rescue a bottle of rum from my place and I told him to bring two. Izzy sighed and let Dawn lead her away. Whatever it was we thought we had to do could wait until morning. That night we needed to be with our friends and neighbours and celebrate our luck at having survived.

***

We didn't last very long: Izzy and I were both exhausted and the food and drink soon had us

89

nodding off. Logan jolted me out of it by suggesting Izzy and I stay with him for the night.

"There's quite a bit of water damage at your place, Duff," Logan told me. "I could see that when I went in for the rum. I had to pick my way through stuff all over floor, from the back door through to the kitchen. The front room is a mess. You don't need to face that tonight. I've got extra rooms, enough for you and Izzy both."

I agreed, again too tired to argue, so we said an early goodbye to the Maddens and set off. But as we walked along to the big house, Logan started going on again about how worried he was about his brother.

"Pete's place should be high enough up in the trees to have escaped the waves—if he made it up to the cabin he's probably fine," I told him.

"Well, I've talked to Rusty Chapman at the fire station," said Logan. "Rusty said no one has been able to get down to the harbour. Both of the roads in are blocked. They know it's taken a beating and Pete and a number of others haven't been seen or heard from since the tsunami hit."

Then he grabbed my arm and looked at me intently, his pale blue eyes brimming with tears.

"Come out with me up to Dingwall tonight," he pleaded. "I have to find Pete and see that he's OK."

"Of course I'll go with you Logan, but we should wait until morning. You don't want to drive the Highlands in the dark after a day like this."

"We have more than an hour of daylight left," argued Logan. "I've driven that part of the Trail dozens of times in the dark, even in winter, and at least then we'll be at the fire station tonight and ready to get into Dingwall at first light."

"Izzy is too tired to go tonight," I argued back, glancing over at my sealing partner.

As I looked back at Logan, I saw that just for a few seconds, the two of them had locked eyes with that spark of sexual intensity that almost always spells trouble. It was so brief I wondered if I'd really seen what I thought I had. But my life depended on paying attention and I was rarely mistaken on things like that. The question was, had this been the first time? Had I missed something going on between them the few times they'd met before Izzy and I'd gone to the ice? Logan wasn't that much older than her so it wasn't unthinkable that they might be attracted to each other. But I didn't think so—this felt like something new.

"I can have a nap in the back on the way," Izzy countered after a short pause. I realized she had somehow repositioned herself and was now standing by Logan's side.

I think she was surprised I hadn't suggested she stay behind. But I wasn't exactly a spring chicken anymore and the whole eye-contact thing aside, even though Logan was young and strong I was sure a third pair of hands and a clear head might come in handy in what lay ahead.

When I argued Izzy and I needed cleaning up, Logan said there were two showers at the house: we could clean up quickly and put on fresh clothes while he rounded up some emergency gear and food. Izzy just raised her eyebrows at me, so I shrugged a grudging agreement and we went into the house.

I noticed Luke's eyes lingering ever-so-slightly longer than necessary on Izzy's form as she trudged down the hall to the bathroom before he turned towards the kitchen, and just shook my head in wonder. But it did make me look at Izzy in a new light. I realized I'd never really registered how feminine was the long dark hair she kept in a single thick braid or the girlish way her long muscular legs terminated below her waist. Was I really so old I hadn't noticed or had I blocked them out as part of the job?

By the time Izzy was showered and changed, I was in clean clothes helping Logan get the last of the supplies stowed in the back of the jeep. I added our two backpacks, which still had some food and warm clothes in them. Logan jammed in one more plastic jug of water and a jerry can of gas into the back but then had a devil of a time getting the door closed. Izzy threw four pillows and some blankets onto the back seat. We didn't have room for much of anything else, so we headed off. Izzy settled her less-than-tiny frame into a nest she'd made on the short back seat, grunting with discomfort more than a few times. I marveled again at her trust and asked Logan how he planned to get to the Cabot Trail road, with the usual route blocked with ice and debris.

As he pulled out onto Oceanview, he glanced at the rearview mirror into the back seat and said in a quiet voice in deference to Izzy's nap, "I should be able to get through on the foot path that connects the end of Cyril's Drive to the south end of New Haven Road, which should bring us out about mid-way between the hospital and the post office. It's wide enough for a snow machine so the jeep should fit through OK. From there, it's less than a kilometre to the Trail road junction. I think the junction is high enough to have escaped damage."

"The real question," he added, "is whether the last bit of the path has been washed out by the wave or is still covered in ice."

We bumped along as Logan drove across the lawns of the houses on the land-ward side of Cyril, because the road was filled with debris left by the wave surge. A big clump of spruce had more or less protected the entrance of the foot path from being covered in ice but many of the trees were leaning dangerously low to the ground. We managed to squeeze under them and around a few small ice blocks scattered across the first 12 metres or so, but then we were clear. The brush rubbing against the sides of the jeep made an awful racket and although the rest of the path was still snow-covered, there wasn't any tsunami debris in our way.

Despite my fears that the ice had destroyed the New Haven road where we expecting to hook up with it, a wall of ice and debris from shattered homes was visible in the fading light just to the left of us as we came to the end of the path. Logan had stopped the jeep for a moment and shook his head as his headlights sparkled against the buckled ice.

He muttered, "Poor buggers," in a quiet voice. I had nothing to add. Then he put the jeep in gear and made a right turn. New Haven was clear all the way to the Trail road junction, which meant we were on our way to Dingwall.

The Cabot Trail Road twists up from the south end of Neil's Harbour into the hills of the Cape Breton Highlands, passing the region's high school above the junction. The highway through the Highlands was well up and back from the coast and given the circumstances, those were two things in our favour. But we had another problem. Logan mentioned that he'd called the fire chief again to let him know we were coming and had been reminded there was some fresh snow on the highway through the Highlands and with the plowed banks over parts of the highway were still over 3 metres high, he would need to take it slow.

I grabbed a pillow that had been ejected from Izzy's nest and set it up against the window so I could rest my eyes for a few moments. I decided not to worry about Logan's driving: he knew the road as well as I did and I trusted him to get us there in one piece. I just needed a few minutes rest. I must have gone under completely, because when I came to less than an hour later, Logan was just pulling to a noisy stop on the highway, well short of the fire station above Dingwall. I'd slept through the usual winter delays—one stop to shovel off the remains of a snow bank that had given way and another to persuade a moose to leave the road—only to be awakened by Logan's loud cursing.

There was a tsunami-sized holdup right ahead that neither Logan or I had thought of: ice blocks and water-driven debris covered the road where it dipped down to the coast at the southernmost harbour in Aspy Bay. The highway was impassible, which meant the whole of South Harbour was probably covered in ice rubble. Which also meant, I then realized, that Middle Harbour next to it would almost certainly be similarly inundated with ice—and that the highway that ran along the lowlands at the back of Middle Harbour, where it met the back road into the town of Dingwall, would be impassible as well.

I can't say, even now, why we hadn't thought of this as a possibility before we set out: Logan and I both knew South and Middle Harbours were 'harbours' in name only. They were really more like huge brackish lagoons and both were surrounded by low-lying ground that tended to swamp in many areas. North and Dingwall Harbours were the only two deep enough for serious boat traffic. I guess we had focused so intently on our destination that some of the realities of the route to the fire station had simply slipped our minds.

However, there was no sense in beating ourselves up about it. Not only were we thoroughly stuck, but all this ice did not bode well for the survival of Logan's brother Pete or the rest of the folks living in Dingwall. Or, for that matter, the continued existence of the town of Aspy Bay, where the region's only elementary school was located.

***

I reached around and jiggled Izzy's leg. Logan got out and just stood by his open door. I opened my door and walked stiffly around to the other side of the jeep while Izzy unfolded herself out of the back and worked her kinks out. She did not seem to realize the problem at first, as she struggled into her parka and moved to stand beside Logan. However, realization registered on her face soon after her eyes shifted up and ahead.

"What the hell...," she muttered, looking around wildly. But the only place we could really see was straight ahead: a huge pile of ice debris covering the road illuminated by the jeep's headlights.

"What are we going to do?" she asked, looking pointedly at me.

"Don't ask me—this was Logan's idea."

She turned her eyes on Logan, who gazed silently out over the ice for a few more minutes then pulled out his phone. Izzy and I waited to see who he was trying to reach. I thought perhaps his brother, but I was wrong. He put the phone on speaker.

"Hey, Rusty," said Logan in an overly calm, steady voice. "This is Logan. We're in a bit of trouble out here. The road's washed out at South Harbour. The highway is impassible, absolutely covered in ice rubble."

Logan and I both knew Rusty well from our many trips back to Dingwall to visit Pete and support the community when they had a fund-raiser, dance, or festival. The fire station was located on the highway above Dingwall, up in the Highlands proper, and Rusty was the fire chief.

"Hi Logan. Yeah, I know about the ice. I tried to call you earlier but the network was down and I couldn't get through. I think your best bet is to back up a bit and go down the White Point Road. I got a call from Hugh McDonald, who lives in the first house on the left there and he said the whole area below him on the South Harbour is covered in ice. He said he'd take you lot in for the night, all three of you. I'm trying to get a helicopter out to pick you up in the morning, on your tab if you don't mind. It can take you out to Dingwall to see if you can find Pete and scout out the situation. I'm hoping you'll get a good enough look around to let us know if we need to go back for survivors."

"OK, Rusty, thanks for all that. If I don't hear from you I'll expect a chopper in the morning at McDonald's place. Good luck with that."

Logan sighed and looked over at me. I shrugged my shoulders and said to Izzy, "Back in the jeep, girl. We've got to find us a place to sleep tonight."

We all climbed back in and Logan got the jeep turned around. We headed a short distance back up the way we'd come to the junction at White Point Road and took a left. Several minutes down that road and we could see lights from what must have been McDonald's house on the left. Logan pulled into the circular drive and parked in front of the big white house. A big burly man, even bigger than me, came out on the front porch to greet us. He had sandy-coloured hair and a short red beard. He wore a suede shearling coat pulled over a red plaid shirt, jeans and pointed boots—the clothes of a farmer, not a fisherman.

"Powers out here and there, not everyone has a generator," Hugh said by way of a greeting, pulling on his gloves. "We've still got heat and power here. Rusty said to expect you, and you're welcome to stay. A bunch of neighbours are here and we've been watching the TV coverage about what's been going on, as much as they know so far anyway."

"We heard it was bad," I said. "This is Logan, and Izzy. I'm Duff. Izzy and I were just coming home into Neil's Harbour from sealing when the tsunami passed underneath us. The noise was something awful. We ended up getting jammed offshore and had to walk home over the ice."

"Sydney seems to be hit the worst but it has to be bad all over," said Hugh. "Grab your stuff and come on in out of the cold. We'll find you something to eat and a place to sleep. Rusty said he would get a helicopter out to pick you up in the morning. He's staying put at the fire station waiting on snow plows to get through from Chéticamp and they're not expected until noon tomorrow."

We all followed Hugh inside. But we only made it through as far as the entry to the living room, where the television was on. There were about eight people scattered around the room and they all looked over briefly as we trouped into the

100

doorway but their eyes immediately swung back to the screen. I've seen all of the news reports since then, of course, of what happened in Sydney. But the images I saw that night on the news of the unbelievable destruction those tsunami waves caused as they ran up Sydney Harbour under the winter ice are still the ones I remember most vividly.

The announcer was saying how much worse this was than the tsunami that had hit the Burin back in 1929 and showed some pictures from back then—a house floating in the harbour, shattered fish stages, homes knocked off their foundations, devastated families standing on the shore looking totally lost, relief trains full of supplies heading out from St. John's. It was a long-gone era, snapshots of a brutally hard way of life few could comprehend in this century. Yet these were people ravaged by the sea because they lived snuggled up to the ocean like a barnacle on a rock—and here we were in the same predicament. A picture of a wooden home shattered by the 1929 wave was shown next to a picture of the enormous reinforced steel inter-island ferry sitting crumpled beyond recognition at its North Sydney dock. It was mind-boggling to fathom the power required to do that kind of damage, let alone comprehend how many lives had been lost. The rest of the images from the city were noteworthy for the lack of familiar landmarks. No steam tower from the power plant at the mouth of the harbour or waterfront houses along the shore into town. No buildings downtown at all—no museums, no office towers, no apartment blocks, no homes—just a huge expanse of ice. It left me feeling hollow.

We all watched in silence for a good ten minutes until Hugh walked in and turned off the set. He asked his wife Meg to put the kettle on. That got the women in the room moving into the kitchen and we all followed.

***

After a tea of biscuits, ham and cheese, I thanked Meg for the meal and headed off to the other side of the kitchen to find Hugh as Izzy tagged along behind me.

"Did Rusty say anything more about the situation in Dingwall?" I asked him quietly when I got him separated from a group of his neighbours.

"Only a little," he said, as Logan joined us. "There seems to be a few pockets of survivors that managed to get out before the waves destroyed their homes. The folks living well back of St. Joseph's Church at the head of the harbour—pretty much all those above the Dingwall Crossroad—seem to be OK but the church itself and the post office on the waterfront are gone. So is Dingwall Road at that end. But another bunch of houses up behind Quarry road on the north side of the harbour are OK. Everyone seemed to be in shock, Rusty said, so he told them all to stay where they were at for the time being and make sure they had enough heat, food, and water to keep themselves going for a few days.

"No one has tried to get out to the boat dock—Jimmy McKay, who lives on the north side well up and back from the waterfront, said he can usually see the old St. Paul Island lighthouse and its museum from his house across the bay but he can't anymore, so he's not optimistic that any of the houses on the other side of the harbour are still standing."

"Yeah, I was afraid of that," I told him. "We can only hope that Pete and any others down at the dock heard the ice coming in and got to higher ground in time. But we won't know for sure until we get a chopper out there."

"Did anyone from this harbour survive?" asked Izzy, looking anxiously over at Hugh. "From South Harbour, I mean. Do you know?"

"It sounds pretty much a repeat of Dingwall, from what we've heard so far. Pockets of survivors hanging on at the fringe of an unbelievable expanse of thick sea ice rubble that's covering all the low land. We have a chopper of our own coming in tomorrow. I guess we'll see then how many folks got buried by the ice and how many made it out alive."

"I don't think I'm going to be able to sleep much tonight," Izzy said in a defeated voice as she kept her eyes focused on the floor rather than Hugh's eyes, which glistened with held-back tears. Logan had somehow ended up beside her and she turned and laid her forehead against his upper arm in an expression of despair and intimacy I'd never seen from her before.

"Let's get our beds made up anyway and lay down," I said, laying a hand gently on her shoulder. "Tomorrow will be a long day and you need some rest even if you don't sleep."

As I turned to go, Logan reached over and cupped Izzy's chin in his great maw of a hand and looked into her eyes.

"As horrific as this day has been, I don't think I'll have any trouble sleeping at all," he said in a hushed voice. Then he let her go and turned to head down the hallway. "I'm totally knackered," he said over his shoulder. "And I'd bet you a dollar that Duff is too, just too proud to say so."

It turned out Logan was right. But before I conked out I did lay awake for a good two minutes wondering what we might find tomorrow. I didn't spare a single thought to what was going on between Logan and Izzy because I knew I couldn't stop it if I tried.

Chapter 6

Hugh woke us just before dawn with the news our chopper was on its way. We had less than an hour to eat and get ready. By the time we got to the kitchen, Meg and Hugh were laying out a meal of muffins, toast, scrambled eggs and coffee. I was so intent on eating I was only vaguely aware of Izzy's sidelong glances at Logan, who was as involved in his meal as I was.

After we ate we saw that Meg had packed us an enormous lunch of ham sandwiches, apples and muffins. "Don't know what you're facing out there," she said matter-of-factly after I thanked her for her kindness. "Just as well you don't have to worry about being hungry on top of everything else."

Logan and Izzy went off to get their gear together, one backpack apiece. Hugh helped me put together an extra bag with rope, crosscut saw, monkey wrench, and crowbar. He threw in a blowtorch and lighter at the last minute, shrugging his shoulders when I raised an eyebrow. I unbuckled my rifle from my backpack and found it just fit into the long cylindrical bag. I wasn't sure what the rules were about taking firearms onto the helicopter and figured what the pilots didn't know might avoid an argument I didn't want to lose.

We heard the chopper coming before we saw it and headed outside to the field beside the house where Hugh had instructed the pilot to land. A much larger helicopter than I had expected, it was painted silver with two red and white stripes across the body and a Canadian flag logo near the tail on each side.

As we loaded ourselves and gear on board, one of the two pilots let us know that a chopper big enough for our needs hadn't been available among the tourist operators of Charlottetown, so some enterprising soul had called across the channel to the Canadian government's Department of Fisheries and Oceans in Moncton, New Brunswick. They had a new Airbus research helicopter that would do the job and were happy to help out at no cost, given the circumstances. It came with two pilots and seats for eight passengers plus floor space that could be used for stretchers if needed. The pilot who had helped us load—whose name, he said, was First Officer Alex Fitzgerald—was also trained in first aid. He introduced the captain as Bob Mayfield and said we needed to put on full-body floatation suits as we were technically scheduled to fly over water, even if it was ice-covered. We pulled on the suits and briefly discussed our plan: fly over the road into Dingwall, assess the damage to the homes and businesses as we went, with our ultimate destination the dock near the mouth of the harbour on the north side.

Captain Bob lifted us off as soon as we were belted in and headed at speed towards Dingwall. I would say we were following the coastline except that there was no coastline to see. The sight from the air took my breath away. I'd never seen Aspy Bay from above but I knew this was not how it usually looked.

"Oh my god," whispered Izzy slowly.

Below us covering the coast road headed northwest was the ice rubble we knew about but what caught us off guard was the scene of destruction that stretched for forever out the other window of the chopper. What should have been a long shallow harbour with scattered houses along the edge was nothing but a field of ice blocks the size of trucks and buses. The White Point Road along the south shore was buried along with any homes or businesses on that coast, and the barrier spit that should have been visible where the harbour met the sea had simply vanished. There was only ice. As we flew, we could see that a long strip of tree-covered high ground still separated South Harbour from its northern neighbour, Middle Harbour. Middle Harbour was filled with ice right up to the Cabot Trail highway and the short barrier spit that normally stretched across its mouth was similarly nowhere to be seen. Dingwall was coming up ahead and would be visible on the horizon within seconds.

When I glanced over I saw Logan place his hands on his thighs and close his eyes for a few seconds to prepare himself for the sight. Izzy briefly covered his right hand with her left but removed it as she and I both leaned over to get a better look out the window.

***

The town of Dingwall was serviced by two roads coming off the highway that went along either side of the bay all the way to the Cabot Strait. Dingwall Road, which was the main entrance, led into the centre of town and then along the south side of the bay out to the south breakwater. Quarry Road went out along the north side of town and on

109

to the commercial boat dock on the north side of the bay. Beyond the dock, Quarry Road went over a stone and concrete breakwater-like barrier that effectively separated Dingwall bay from North Harbour. It then continued across an uninhabited bit of ground covered in scrubby spruce which soon turned into the sand that made up the southern base of the barrier spit across North Harbour. From there, Quarry Road continued out to the base of the man-made breakwater.

Vast stretches of the upper part of Dingwall Road were now covered by ice and debris pushed up by the tsunami waves that had inundated the area of low-lying land behind Middle Harbour. Even though it was well back from the water, the first kilometre or so of the Dingwall Road ran along the northern edge of this low patch of ground and now, all but a few high spots had been obliterated by water and ice by a tsunami sneak-attack-from-the-side. The rest of the Dingwall Road into town had been just high enough to keep it intact.

However, as we came closer we could see that the Quarry Road just a bit further north—which at first had looked clear—was blocked for a short distance where the ice plowing in from Middle Harbour had surged the furthest north. The turnoff from the Cabot Trail onto Quarry Road was only a short distance north of the Dingwall Road junction but that road ran mostly along high ground from the highway to the old gypsum mine, which had been closed for many decades by that time. But then it dipped down in one vulnerable spot before rising up again to follow the ridge to the far side of town, where it dropped down to sea level near the head of the harbour. It was that one low point between the quarry and town that had been hit by the tsunami-driven ice.

Dingwall proper, population about 500 at that time, lay at the head of Dingwall Harbour. The St. Joseph's Parish Church was a major landmark that sat well back from the water's edge, a bit south of town. Its spire came into view in the distance as Captain Bob turned the chopper north and we flew towards town above the Dingwall Road.

"At least the church is still standing," said Logan softly. "That's something."

As we approached the church, people poured out of the building, thirty or so at my best guess. Captain Bob did a little wobble to acknowledge their waves then turned northeast towards town. Once he flew over Dingwall he would need to veer to the north again and follow the Quarry Road along the north shore to the boat dock.

However, the sight of what should have been Dingwall shocked us all.

"Where the hell is it?" said Alex muttered into the microphone attached to his helmet.

"We can only hope most of them got out alive," I said. "Might account for some of those folks at the church."

Dingwall no longer existed. An enormous ridge of ice had been pushed against the forest that had once marked the back edge of the town. This ridge of ice was higher than the ridge we had seen at Neils Harbour but like that one, its leading edge was embedded with the leftovers of the town's human existence: a peaked roof here, a crushed truck there, bits of broken lumber and concrete everywhere. It was an exaggerated picture of the one that had greeted us at Neils Harbour the day before.

It just broke my heart. There was a long silence as we hovered over the destruction below, broken finally by Captain Bob asking over his headset if we wanted to land and take a look around. I looked over at Logan, who responded in an oddly flat voice, "No, just go on ahead to the dock. We can stop on the way back if we need to."

So the captain made a long sweeping turn to head along the north side of the harbour. The

112

part of the Quarry Road that had once connected the town to the boat dock was gone: there was nothing but ice rubble from tree-line to tree-line where once people's homes had lined the water. The same kind of ridge of tsunami-driven ice that we'd seen at Dingwall was a new feature of the landscape below: ice and debris driven into a wall against a barrier of trees left standing only because decades before they had taken root on slightly higher ground. Nothing could be seen of the homes and the museum that once stood on the south side of the harbour along Dingwall Road: they had all been built on low-lying land and now their crushed remains were resting up against the forest within a mountain ridge of ice.

None of this bode well for the survival of anyone who had been out near mouth of the harbour when the tsunami hit. The land was barely above sea level and the low breakwater across the mouth that protected the boat dock behind it would not have slowed down the incoming waves. I could see reality setting in on Logan's face. Even if Pete had heard the deafening roar of the tsunami in time to get out of his boat and off the dock, would he have been able to out-run the advancing ice? Could he really have made it all the way to his cabin in the trees before it was too late?

***

"You'll have to let me know where you want me to set down," shouted Captain Bob, interrupting our worried thoughts. "There are no landmarks for me to aim for."

"Just in front of that last patch of trees," said Logan into his headset, looking out the left window. "The dock would have been more or less in front of that bit of forest. Pete and his friend Tommy Martell each have a little cabin up in those woods but there's only a trail into them, not a real road."

Captain Bob nodded and swung the helicopter around for a landing on the flattest piece of ice-covered landscape he could find, which turned out to be a greater distance from the trees than we might have liked. As the chopper turned, I caught movement down below out the corner of my eye, but when I looked more closely I didn't see anything. Probably a shadow, I thought. But then Izzy, who was looking out the opposite window, gave a shout.

"Hey! I see tracks," she called out. "I think somebody must be alive down there. Do you see them Duff?"

"Barely. Wind must have picked up ice crystals over night and blew them around. It hasn't snowed out here, at any rate. That's a blessing."

"I'll have to set down over in that flattish spot to the south of those tracks," Captain Bob told us. "Alex and I will have to stay with the chopper. While you're looking around we'll prepare a triage area onboard in case you find anyone injured we need to transport."

I gave him a thumbs-up as the machine hovered briefly before making its descent. Bob expertly settled the chopper into a small patch of level ice with hardly a bump. We unbuckled our harnesses and grabbed our bags as the screaming rotors wound to a halt. Alex moved into the cabin to open the cargo door and lower the boarding steps. As quickly as we could, Logan, Izzy and I got ourselves and our gear off-loaded. We got out of our survival suits and passed them over to the pilots.

"Good luck," shouted Alex. "If you're not back in four hours we'll come looking for you. But it would be better if we didn't have to. Do you have the flares?"

Logan gave him a thumbs-up and we all turned to walk towards the trees—in the direction where Izzy had seen the tracks and where we hoped we'd find some evidence that Pete was still alive.

***

Logan led the way with Izzy next in line and me straggling behind. We each had a sealing gaff to help us over the broken ice but it was still a difficult march. I finally had to shout ahead for them to slow down.

"I'm not as good at scrambling over these damn ice blocks as the two of you," I bellowed at them, struggling to catch my breath. "I'd just as soon not break my neck trying to keep up, thank you very much."

I saw Izzy stop and looked back at me as I worked my way over yet another treacherous mound. When next I looked up I realized she had turned back around but was looking into the distance, off to her left.

"What the hell is that?" she shouted. "Over there near the trees." Logan and I both turned and looked in the direction she was pointing. I had to squint to find what she was seeing and kicked myself for not thinking to bring the binoculars. It wasn't all that far but there was a lot of glare coming off the ice. I expected to see a survivor coming out from shore to meet us but that wasn't what it was. At least, I didn't think so. It just didn't seem the right shape and it wasn't moving the right way for a person.

"Is that a bear?" asked Logan from the top of an icy ridge, as Izzy and I caught up with him.

"I think it must be," I answered. "A big black bear."

"Maybe those tracks we saw from the chopper were him walking around on the ice," suggested Izzy.

"That would make more sense than a person wandering around out here," Logan replied with a just a bit too much bite in his voice. Again with the eye contact between the two of them but this time it wasn't sexually electric but argumentative, and Izzy's face distorted into a scowl. Logan was definitely on edge, which wasn't usual for him—just as it was unusual for her to take offense at such an offhand remark.

But before Izzy could erupt at Logan's dismissive comment, I pointed again at the bear. They both turned to see the bear standing up on its hind legs and looking off in the distance. Not at us but off to our right, along what would have been the shoreline before the tsunami hit. We looked in the direction he was looking but couldn't see anything. Within seconds he dropped back onto all fours and ran off at a gallop in the other direction, leaping over the ice rubble as fast as he could.

"That's odd," I said quietly. "Something sure got him spooked. But there's nothing else out here that I can see except us and he didn't seem aware we were even here."

"Well, let's keep going," urged Logan, clambering down into the valley between the ridge we'd been standing on and the low mound of buckled ice ahead. "Pete's cabin should be in that little patch of trees over there to the right, so let's head over there and see what we can find."

I didn't argue, so off we trudged towards that part of the scrubby spruce forest, if you could call it that. The spooked-bear incident had rattled me and I really wanted the rifle in my hand. But Logan was carrying the extra bag that had the gun in it and had again surged ahead, way in front of Izzy. I again hollered at him to slow down. He gave me an impatient glance and I thought I saw him curse through clenched teeth but he did comply. Izzy shot me a grateful nod.

After several minutes of climbing over ice that reminded me of photos in a newspaper of the worst kind of pile-up of vehicles on a foggy highway, we came to the back side of the final ridge that had been pushed up against the higher ground near the woods. It was close to 18 metres tall in places but at least the shattered ice seemed to be frozen firmly in place. I took a deep breath to steady my nerves as Logan and Izzy prepared to go up over the top.

***

From my position behind them I could see a gap in the ice off to my left. Logan and Izzy had been walking so fast and with such purpose that they had missed it.

"Hang on, you two. There's a gap over this way that will be way easier than climbing that damn mountain."

They both stepped back down from the base of the ice ridge and walked along to meet me at the gap. There was still some ice but not as much as there was on either side. Once there I could see a huge boulder had blocked the forward movement of the ice ridge. There had been such a rock offshore before the tsunami, in back of the dock. It never got in the way of boats because it was near shore, well away from the main channel.

Walking up and over the ice piled around the gap, we could see that for a length of more than 30 metres north of us, the base of the ice ridge contained a mess of broken timbers from the boat

119

dock and storage shed, toppled trees, shattered lobster traps, and chunks of broken boat parts—with a few brightly-painted trucks mixed in. The chopper hadn't flown over the tree line before we'd set down on the ice, so we hadn't had any forewarning of the extent of destruction. After having seen what had happened to the town of Dingwall, this wasn't much of a surprise. But it was still a shock. I think perhaps we had all hoped against odds that something had turned the tables so that the damage out here would be at least a little bit less. Logan's fallen face reflected the disappointment and loss I felt.

Izzy seemed to be taking it in stride but then, she hadn't known the Dingwall dock and its community the way we had. Rory McInnis and the way he could spin a story; Billy Young, always the optimist no matter the trouble; Benji Bates, baby brother of my sealing partner Jimmy, sharing around the cakes his mum baked every Tuesday; old Sam Forbes, always cursing and fiddling with that ancient engine of his; Neil Gallant, like me the only sealer among a dock full of lobstermen. And of course, Logan's brother Pete Wilkie and his mate Tommy Martell, who had fished for lobster out of this harbour as long as I'd known him.

It looked like the sea had run up under the ice well into the patch of trees before it had retreated. There was a relatively clear path about 10 metres wide between the front of the berm and the higher ground of the trees. Fortunately, the tsunami backwash had not frozen along this stretch, because otherwise we would have had a dangerous walk along a slippery slope.

Without saying anything, Logan set off north along the berm edge, stopping occasionally to look at some of the debris embedded in the ice. He shook his head sadly and pointed as he spotted a fragment of Sam's old blue and white boat, a chunk of the bow with the first three letters of its name sticking out of the ice above his head. Up ahead of him, an artificial point of sorts had formed. A massively-dented but still bright yellow long-box pickup truck stuck so far out of the ice berm it almost touched the forest edge. Logan headed around it as Izzy and I lagged behind.

We heard a sudden cry of anguish from Logan. As we ran around the truck, we saw he had fallen to his knees. Less than ten metres in front of him along the berm edge lay the body of a man dressed in jeans, deck boots and a red and black coat ripped to tatters over the torso. An enormous polar bear stood over it. The bear had raised its great head at the intrusion, showing his blood-covered face.

Logan let out another wail and the bear glared at him. It was fat and stood taller than any bear I'd ever seen. The animal made a peculiar hissing sound that startled Logan into silence. As he got to his feet, the bear charged.

The bear rushed forward almost 3 metres. As Logan scrambled backwards, the bear pulled to a sudden stop. Izzy and I grabbed Logan's arms and hauled him back behind the truck, where he crumpled to the ground again, moaning and muttering Pete's name over and over. It had all happened so fast I hadn't had time to even think about the rifle, let alone get it out of the bag. My heart was pounding so fast I thought it might stop.

"How do you know?" Izzy demanded. "How can you be sure?"

"The jacket," I said in a low voice. "Logan gave him that for Christmas, ordered from Norway. Not a one like it on the dock."

I just shook my head as Izzy held him, stroking his head and making soothing sounds as you would with a toddler in distress.

I told Izzy to stay with him. I unzipped the duffle bag and pulled out my rifle, then headed slowly back around the truck. I crossed over to the edge of the trees and made my way north, parallel to the berm edge. I didn't want to get near the bear standing over Pete's body but I had to know what else was going on over there.

***

Beyond the bear busy consuming Pete I could see two more bears that looked to be eating. As I came out from the safety of the trees to get a better look at each of them, the bears raised their heads at me, glaring briefly at the invasion of their space. Whatever, or whoever, they were eating was out of sight from where I stood. But I stayed still for a moment and they did not charge. Soon they each went back to eating, ignoring my rude intrusion.

I moved further along until I got near the end of the dock debris and spotted yet another white bear. Its rump was to me so I couldn't see what he was doing. Half a smashed lobster boat lay between the woods and the berm, so I scurried forward for a better look, taking cover behind the crushed bow. The bear was less than six metres away and I have no idea what madness made me want to get so close.

The wind was toward me and I could smell him: a ripe marine wildness like I'd never known. I could also hear him rip and chew whatever it was he was eating. I felt a need to know and yet guilty for giving in to my curiosity. What was wrong with me? What did it matter? After what I'd already seen, did I think I would see a whale?

I peeked around the edge of my boat blind just as the big white butt started to move. It swung around counterclockwise until its face was pointing towards me. This gave me a better view of the bear and the two bodies it was guarding. Both torsos and thighs were mostly consumed. I was pretty sure it was Benji Bates and his mother Sarah spayed out in the debris with the bear looming over them. The dark-haired body was the right size and shape for Benji and I knew Sarah's seal skin boots, given to her by Jimmy decades ago. Those boots were a regular winter sight at the dock when she came down with that cake tin of hers. She boasted of not having bought a new pair of boots in twenty years, as if it were an important virtue. In truth, I knew she was showing her pride that Jimmy was such a successful sealer he could afford to buy her the best quality boots. Plus, and I honestly think this was the most important reason, they were a daily reminder of her first born who lived away but not too far.

124

All of a sudden, I was overcome with grief and a powerful sense of resentment. What need did these bears have of human flesh when they'd been feeding on whales and seals the whole winter? They were already fatter than any bear I'd ever seen— why had they come ashore here to defile the bodies of my friends who had suffered a tragic death already? It was the added insult of the disfigured bodies that got my anger up. I stepped clear of the boat and raised the rifle. I aimed at the top of the bear's head then kicked the boat to get his attention. As he raised his head to glare at me, I took a deep breath and adjusted my sights to focus on his chest. Slowly, I began to squeeze the trigger as his eyes burned into mine.

But something stopped me from pulling the trigger all the way. Then the opportunity was gone. The bear's enormous head went back down and my target disappeared.

I could lie and say that I had reached a moral decision not to kill the bear but the truth is that I had been afraid—overwhelmingly afraid for the second time in two days. I'd never tried to kill an animal that big before. How many shots would it take? If the first shot didn't kill him, how much time did I have to get in a second—and would he have me by the neck before I was able to get it off?

I remembered again some of the stories John had told me of the ways that polar bears had killed people in Newfoundland last year. They went for the head, he'd said.

And if I killed this bear, surely I should kill all four. Was that even possible before one of them got to me, with them all so close together? The speed at which the first bear had charged Logan had also given me pause. It was hard to believe a bear that big could move so fast. That look in this bear's eye, for just that brief second, now haunted me—it was as if he'd been daring me to shoot, without a shred of fear for himself. And lastly, I wondered—not for the first time in my life—how was it that so many thoughts could fill your head in such a short space of time?

The bear had gone back to his feeding—I was no longer a threat. He'd exposed his heart to me for a few brief seconds and when I hadn't immediately taken advantage, he'd dismissed me. So confident was he in his position at the top of his food chain that my presence didn't concern him. I thought of how cavalierly I had told Izzy, only a few weeks ago, that I would face a charging bear to save her life. What did I think about that now?

Then the bear did something curious. He sat down and wiped his bloody muzzle repeatedly

126

against a nearby ice block, leaving a broad crimson smear. Then he lay down and proceeded to lick his paws clean of the blood of my good friends. The oddly fastidious act somehow settled my mind and I decided I had probably done the right thing. I reminded myself that the tsunami had killed Benji and Sarah—the bear hadn't done the killing. Although I wasn't absolutely sure that was true, it felt OK to assume it was. Then I had a thought that the least I could do was to find out who the two people were that the other bears were feeding on, so that their deaths could be properly recorded.

I moved back to the edge of the woods and made my way back toward the truck that still blocked Izzy and Logan from my sight. As I got to the next bear, whose back was to me, I dared to creep forward enough to see that the body on the ground was Bill Dixon, whose job it was to keep the dock's storage shed in order. The bear had repositioned the body since I had seen it earlier and now Bill's blonde hair was visible against a piece of red-painted lumber from the shed he had devoted himself to. There was such an irony in that picture that it somehow put me at peace, and I moved on.

The second bear had also moved since I'd first seen him. He'd dragged the body he was feeding on closer to the forest, so I had to climb up the slope and work my way through the trees in order to keep any real distance between us. As I got to a point opposite the big bear, I peeked out from behind a spruce to chance a look and saw old Sam's unmistakable beard jammed between a torn-up lifejacket and a block of ice. Nearby, I caught sight of one of Sam's patched-up boots, which had originally been yellow but were now a mosaic of black and silver tape. I said a silent goodbye and moved south until I could safely return to the bare path in front of the ice berm.

I was shortly in front of the mighty bear that had charged at Logan. He had moved away from Pete's body and appeared to be feeding on someone else. It appeared to be a small woman. I thought I saw a patch of short dark hair. It could have been a teenage girl or even a young boy but there was no way to recognize whoever it was. The face was all ripped up and I didn't recognize the clothes. Someone's child, I decided sadly. And then I felt angry all over again for the mutilation of the body.

I raised the gun and fired a shot over the bear's head. He stopped what he was doing and looked up in surprise. I fired again close to his feet. This time he bolted down the beach towards the sea, passing the other bears as he ran. They looked up briefly then went back to feeding.

I lowered the rifle and moved around the truck to where Izzy and Logan were still huddled on the cold, wet ground. They looked up expectantly at me and life returned to Logan's face.

"Did you get him, Duff?" he asked with excitement in his voice. "Did you kill the bastard?"

"I did," I answered after a moment's hesitation. "He's gone."

I don't really know why I lied about killing the bear but it seemed important to Logan that the bear, as well as Pete, was dead. Izzy raised an eyebrow at me and I wondered if she'd heard the bear run off. I turned away rather than respond but she didn't let it go.

"Gone's as good as dead, I guess," she said quietly but looking me straight in the eye. "So much for lessons learned from the mistakes of others."

I was sure Logan hadn't heard her because a small contended smile came across his face.

"Yes!!" he said, as his face filled with triumph for a brief moment. Then he seemed to remember why it mattered and collapsed back into himself.

"Let's get out of here," I said as I tucked the rifled back in the duffle out of sight. "We got what we came for. We should get back to the chopper."

Izzy nodded and helped Logan to his feet. But when he got upright, Logan started to protest that he wanted to take Pete's body home. I'd been afraid he might do that and wasn't looking forward to trying to talk him out of it. I was sure he didn't need to see close-up evidence of the bear's mutilation. But just as I was about to speak, we heard a shout. We all turned and saw two figures emerge from the trees a bit south of where we stood.

"Help!" one of them shouted, waving his arms. "Over here!"

Chapter 7

We all ran as fast as we could down the tsunami-washed path in front of the ice berm to where the two people were standing. I saw as I got closer that the person who'd been shouting was Tommy Martell, Pete's mate. The other looked like Dougie Robinson but I couldn't be sure. Dougie did maintenance work for the Markland resort during the tourist season. All of a sudden, I wondered if the Markland cabins had survived—perhaps the hill they were perch on, out near the harbour mouth, had been high enough to save them.

When we caught up to Tommy, it turned out the person beside him was Dougie's cousin, Carl. Carl had his arm in a rough sling and a bandage wound around his head. Logan fairly flung himself in Tommy's arms and muttered that Pete was dead.

"Yes, well, I figured as much. As far as we know, no one who was down at the dock when the ice hit made it out. Neil Gallant was still out sealing in the Gulf but we haven't heard from him. Carl here was mending traps above the dock and saw it come in. He watched the wave of ice set to smash the boats and hammer all the men running down the dock trying to get out of the way. He turned and ran, managed to get out in front of it but fell and hit his head as he was running through the woods. I was up there by myself in the cabin, working on the little rowboat I'd promised my grandson. I heard it coming, of course. I was running that way to see what it was when I found Carl out cold with a dislocated shoulder. When he came to I ran down to the beach to get a quick look but there was no beach. No beach, no dock, no boats, no shed, nothing—nothing but ice and debris as far as I could see. It was pretty clear no one out there had got out alive.

"I went back to tend to Carl and got him to the cabin. A few minutes after I got Carl bound up, Mike Burke comes running in, screaming that his wife Ellen had been hurt bad. Mike and Ellen lived up the Quarry Road about half way to Dingwall. They'd been driving out to the dock to deliver some boat parts to Billy Young before heading over to their daughter's place on the south shore to help with the new baby. Mike could see the ice coming up the harbour but realized there was nothing he could do to avoid it. The ice smashed into the car, then picked it up, turned it over, and slammed it against a tree. Mike wasn't much hurt and was able to get out by himself but Ellen was pinned inside. It took us hours with a crowbar to get her out. Her left arm is pretty badly mangled but I got her trussed up as best I could manage. I'm pretty sure her shoulder and elbow are both broken and need to be properly set. She's also in a lot of pain and really needs a doctor."

"We can take her in the chopper," I said. "All of you, in fact. We came out here looking for Pete. But he's already gone. We found his body at the edge of that ridge of ice piled up against the shore. Sam Forbes too, as well as Benji and Sarah Bates. And a kid I didn't recognize. The rest who were out at the dock must be buried under the ice."

Izzy looked like she was going to say something about the polar bears so I interrupted to stop her blurting something out. Any mention of bears eating people would just get Logan all wound up again and we didn't need his anguish on top of his grief at losing Pete. Right now we had another job to do.

"We don't have time or the strength to take bodies out," I said pointedly. "We'll have trouble

133

enough getting two injured people over that broken ice. Let's go to the cabin, collect the Burkes, and see if we can figure out how to best get all of us safely onto that chopper. "

Tommy and Carl both nodded their heads in agreement, and after a brief hesitation Izzy and Logan did the same. The walk through the scrubby woods was blissfully short and in less than five minutes the trail opened up to a clearing around a small rough-built log cabin. Tommy hollered for Mike, who almost immediately opened the door.

"I was just coming to look for you," he said to Tommy as we all crowded around the entrance. He was clearly distressed—two big teardrops welled in the corners of his big brown eyes. "Ellen is starting to scream with the pain. We've got to get her to a doctor."

"These folks came in a helicopter and offered to take us all out with them," Tommy told him. "Come and help me get Ellen ready to go. She's going to have to walk once we get out of the woods because the ice is too broken up to carry her over it but let's see if we can make her as comfortable as possible for the first part of the trip out of here."

As Tommy and Mike headed inside, I had an idea that might allow Ellen to tolerate the pain I

134

knew she would have to endure. I pulled out my phone and dialed the number that Alex, the first officer, had given me.

"Alex, this is Duff. We have a problem here. We've found a badly injured survivor we are going to walk back to the chopper. But she's in a lot of pain. Is there any chance you could meet us half way and give her a shot of morphine or something? She might be more willing to set out if we can promise her some relief."

"Roger, Duff, I was just going to call you. We were getting worried. I can certainly grab a bag and meet you. Where should I be aiming for?"

"We're a bit south of our original destination. Give us 30 minutes or so to get out to the edge of the trees and we'll send up a flare. You send up one from your position and we'll hopefully meet somewhere in between. We'll have three additional survivors with us, including one with a shoulder injury, so four extra altogether. We should be pretty easy to spot."

"Roger, Duff, I think that will work. Did you find Pete?"

"Yeah, we found him but he was dead. No one out on the dock survived."

135

"Hell, Duff, that's a pity. I'm sure sorry to hear that but he would have needed a miracle to have survived this."

"Yeah, the ice really had a field day out here. We're bringing back the only miracles we could find."

"Roger, Duff, I'll pack my things and head out. Meet you shortly."

As I disconnected, I saw Izzy pull out one of the flares we'd been given from the duffle bag. I gave her a quick nod and suggested she and Carl head back to the edge of the woods with the duffle bag. They could set off the flare from there as soon as they arrived. We'd need Logan's strength to get Ellen out as fast as possible—if we could get him to respond.

***

Ellen was a pudgy red-head whose face under her freckles was now almost white from the pain she'd been enduring. She had insisted she was most comfortable sitting up, so Mike and Tommy settled on securing her to a high-backed wooden chair with some rope and torn strips of sheeting so we could carry the chair, rather than her body. I didn't think that would work going over the ice but it would get us over the trail faster than her

136

walking. We thought of putting her in the utility hand cart Pete and Tommy used to haul supplies but realized it was too wide for us to keep the chair steady in its bucket. It turned out to be easier for the four of us to simply lift and carry the chair, one at each leg. Mike wasn't a big man but he was pretty strong. Luckily, Logan was able to carry out this simple physical activity when I told him what to do but he still had an odd, blank look on his face. Shortly after we set off down the path we heard the bang from Izzy's flare. It startled Ellen, who was already a bit disconcerted to be so high in the air, and the pain of her movement set her off crying. But I reminded her again that we had a first aid officer coming to meet us and he would have the morphine she needed. She bit her lip and nodded she was ready, so off we went. She didn't even whimper after that, at least not that I could hear.

And in the end, however, Ellen objected strenuously to being taken off her chariot when we finally got to the ice. She took one look at the massive ridge in front of us and insisted she couldn't possibly climb over it, even with all of us helping. So we left her rigged up and gave it a try. To my surprise, the chair-fix worked better than expected. It took all of us to do it but with two pulling up on the back of the chair as the other two pushed from the bottom, we were able to get Ellen over that first enormous ridge without too much trouble. She moaned a few times but was remarkably brave about it. Carl almost had a harder time, since he had only one good arm to climb with, but with Izzy's help he was able to manage.

After a half an hour of this effort, we heard a loud bang and saw another flare shoot into the air over to our right. It wasn't very far from us but we couldn't see Alex because of some giant blocks of ice between us. I wasn't sure he'd be able to hear us if we shouted, so I nodded to Izzy, who dug out another one of our flares and fired it off.

We were in a comfortable place to take a rest, so I suggested we wait for Alex to find us. We passed around the water bottles but kept as quiet as we could. Within five minutes we could hear him calling.

"Over here," I shouted. "We're waiting for you."

And then we could see his red survival suit up ahead, clambering over the ice.

Mike gave Ellen a kiss on the forehead for being so brave. She tried to smile but it come more like a grimace. But we could see she was relieved.

Alex got right to work examining Ellen's arm and made short work of giving her the promised morphine shot. Then he looked up and noticed Carl's sling.

"You need one of these too?"

"Nah, I'm OK—I've been putting ice on it since yesterday, since there was so much of it about," he said with a cheeky grin.

We all shook our heads at his attempt at a joke. Alex started walking back and forth around our little rest area and it dawned on me that he was pacing it off. I opened my mouth to speak but he beat me to it.

"I bet Bob could land the chopper here if you all move out of the way," he said. "It would be tight but would save all of us having to climb all the way back over this damn ice. You'll have to go back over that ridge there and wait for Bob to set it down, but I think it could work."

He pulled out his phone and got Bob to agree to give it a try. With a groan, we climbed back the way we had come to give the chopper space to land. Alex sat at the top of the ridge to help direct Bob into the hole. It would only work because the surrounding ice peaks were much lower than the rotors.

Within a few minutes we heard the powerful engines start up. Soon the chopper appeared overhead. Slowly, Captain Bob set the

139

machine down between the ice ridges and turned the rotors off. Alex scaled down the slope as Bob got the door open. Alex made sure the boarding steps were secure at the bottom then waved us forward. Ellen was loaded on first and then Carl. The rest of us waited while the two injured survivors were secured inside, then Alex waved the rest of us aboard and we put our survival suits back on.

I put my helmet on and adjusted the headphones, then heaved a sigh of relief as Bob took the chopper back up. But as he spun the machine around to head south and hovered there for a moment, I looked out the window toward North Harbour and saw nothing but an endless expanse of ripped up ice. I was overwhelmed with sadness for all those lost in the town of Aspy Bay, which was as low-lying as Dingwall. Still, I was thankful the tsunami had hit on a Sunday morning because the school house in Aspy Bay would have been empty.

The rest of the passengers in the chopper appeared lost in thought, looking blankly ahead or at their feet. Izzy, seated across from me, was holding Logan's hand. But I was still looking out the window. I imagined I saw four polar bears with bloody faces looking up at the chopper overhead.

***

After a few minutes, Captain Bob's voice came through the headphone.

"We'll head straight to the hospital at Neil's Harbour so that Mrs. Burke can be attended to. Logan, you'll have to pick up your vehicle later."

Logan didn't respond so I gave Bob a thumbs-up and settled in for the short ride over the highlands. But when I glanced over at Izzy, I saw she was looking at me with a quizzical expression on her face. When she saw me looking, she raised that familiar eyebrow at me. I shook my head ever so slightly and saw her turn away.

It had broken, I realized—that bond between us based on trust and straight talk. The sealing lessons she'd come for were long over, of course, so there was really no reason for our relationship to continue. Except it would have done, I knew, if not for what had happened today. We'd have crossed paths after months or years and felt comfortable with each other as good friends do, if only today hadn't happened. I'd spoiled it. It wasn't just the lie I'd told back on the ice but my refusal to talk to the others about the polar bears we'd seen—to tell the story straight.

The moment had arrived for me to make that right—I could have suggested Bob take the chopper back over the area where the bodies were scattered and talked about what had happened. But I'd let that moment come and go. And then every minute afterwards that I stayed silent made it all the harder to say anything at all. In those few moments, I'd got caught in a vicious loop that kept me silent all these years.

I told myself at the time that Logan's grief would only deepen and linger if he dwelled on the horrific sight of the polar bear devouring his brother—that talking about it would so cement the vision in his mind that it would be there forever. I told myself I was trying to be kind and if challenged, I knew that's how I would have defended my actions.

But I knew it wasn't the main reason. I'd faced a new level of fear that day that I hadn't known how to accept. That look of defiant power in the eyes of that last bear had changed me somehow. Robbed me of the confidence I counted on: self-confidence I thought I'd earned through years of facing life-threatening events. I was pretty sure I'd done the right thing by not pulling the trigger on that bear but I was beginning to feel damn sure I'd done the wrong thing by not talking to Izzy about it.

I should have been able to say those things out loud. Facing the challenges of life is how we learn and it had been my way to share what I'd learned, because it could help someone else get out of a jam without dying. It's part of what stories were for. It was why Jimmy had sent Izzy to me in the first place—I had a reputation for teaching. I knew it made me uncomfortable to know that Izzy had seen this weakness but I didn't quite know why. Maybe if there'd been a quiet moment out there to talk with Izzy about the bears, I might have figured it out. She might have asked me what had happened after I'd fired the shots but she was so busy comforting Logan that she hadn't bothered to take me aside to demand some answers. Did I resent that?

Maybe I did. Her obvious attraction to Logan had made me aware that Izzy was a woman as much as she was a competent scaling partner. It felt a little like broken trust or maybe shifted loyalty, but even as I say those things it in my head they sound petty. Still, it was how it felt, unreasonable as it might have been. Our friendship had changed.

I was startled out of my thoughts by a change in the vibration generated by the rotors as Captain Bob started his descent. I looked out and saw the Buchanan Hospital below. We landed uneventfully. When the doors opened there was an explosion of activity getting the injured passengers unloaded and only then were the rest of us allowed off. I climbed down first and waited for the others to join me. But Izzy put her arm around Logan's waist after she helped him down the stairs and led him into the building, passing me without a glance. I knew then I hadn't been wrong about what had happened between us.

Chapter 8

I don't know if Izzy said anything to anyone about the polar bears. I doubt Logan did, so if I didn't tell the story, who would know? Perhaps, now that I think of it, it hadn't been a kindness to deprive Logan of a chance to talk about what had happened. He was in shock for days after we got back to Neil's Harbour. Izzy went home with him to the big house next to mine and I rarely saw them afterwards. Folks came to the house to pay their respects and bring food, but Logan and Izzy didn't go out. After a week or so had passed, and the weather warmed up a bit, I caught a ride out to South Harbour to retrieve Logan's jeep. He came out and thanked me woodenly when I parked it in his driveway but Izzy just looked out in silence from the doorway.

A month passed before there was a funeral for Pete and others who had died that day in Dingwall—in truth, it was one funeral after the next North of Smokey that month and many were held for entire families at once. It turned out the entire Aspy Bay region of Cape Breton had been the worst affected in terms of sheer area of ice rubble covering the land. Many folks caught near the mouths of the low-laying harbours, like Pete, had had the furthest to run to reach higher ground and made up most of the dead. Folks living further back from the outer coast heard the growling thunder of the breaking ice coming closer and sensed the approaching disaster. Having a shorter run to safety, most of them managed to get out alive. But all of their homes, boats, vehicles, and businesses were destroyed. All along the east coast of Cape Breton, communities like Neil's Harbour had less loss of life than Aspy Bay but almost as much property destruction.

Fortunately, electrical power North of Smokey came from a hydro dam up in the Highlands and the many downed power lines along the coast were rather quickly restored—mostly within weeks. There was a lot of work to do cleaning up but it all had to wait until the ice melted. The giant ice ridges filled with debris were frozen into walls as hard as concrete and were the last to melt. There were bodies in that wreckage but also some surprises. When the ice in Neil's Harbour

146

melted, a lens from the lantern belonging to the old lighthouse was found with only two cracks and a few chips out of the glass. There was talk of making a sort of museum display out of it, along with some of the twisted bits of metal and broken red-painted boards that had been recovered from the lighthouse but I don't know if that ever happened.

Almost sixty bodies out in Dingwall were recovered after the ice melted, and more than that in Aspy Bay. Many of these had been partially eaten but the damage was blamed on scavenging black bears, since indeed they were responsible for at least some of the carnage. As the melting ice slowly released the accumulated debris, three big black bears had been shot in Dingwall after they were spotted feeding on the dead.

Only Izzy, Logan, and I knew the black bears weren't responsible for all of that damage. Had there been other polar bears in the other harbours of Aspy Bay in the few days after the tsunami, I wondered, feeding on the people killed by the ice but left exposed in the open? There could have been. I figured that within a few days, without anyone but us knowing they had ever been there, the four polar bears at Dingwall had disappeared over the ice. Eventually, they would have headed back to the coast of Labrador and eventually made their way back to the Arctic. While a few white bears had been spotted out over the Gulf in the weeks after the tsunami by pilots flying rescue operations in and out of Sydney, no one seemed to suspect they had been ashore on Cape Breton in the aftermath of the disaster.

After a few months, Izzy took Logan to central Maine, miles away from ice that could rise up like a monster and an eternity away from the possibility of being devoured by polar bears. I never heard from or saw either of them again, although I thought of them often. Nothing on Cape Breton was ever really the same after that, as hard as people tried. So much had been destroyed. The shoreline was totally rearranged in some places and no one knew who owned what piece of remaining land. Many folks north of Smokey just lost heart and left. So much of Sydney had been destroyed that rebuilding efforts in the city left precious few resources for smaller communities: as always, the urban centre sucked up the sympathy as well as the money. I could barely watch the news.

I did hear a government geologist on the radio a few years later who'd had some straight-talk comments about the event. They stuck with me, maybe because the woman reminded me so much of Izzy in the way she talked. She was astonished, she said, that neither she nor any of her colleagues had ever thought about the possibility that a tsunami might hit while most of Cabot Strait was covered in ice, even though they knew that a repeat of the 1929 Grand Banks tsunami was likely to occur at some point. It had been an extraordinary blind spot and was hard for her to fathom.

If I understood what she said correctly, the presence of the ice had made an enormous difference in the amount of damage. The ice cover transformed the energy of the first tsunami wave so that when it hit the coastline, it literally exploded onto the shore with a destructive power many times greater than that of a regular tsunami of the same size. This meant the water went further and travelled higher. More importantly, it also hurled blocks of broken ice weighing one or two tons at the landscape with tremendous force, crushing or smashing everything they touched. But the second and third waves did something else: those waves *pushed* all that broken ice ashore until they created a huge ridge of almost solid ice that swept even further inland like the blade of a giant bulldozer. She called it an 'ice shove'. With colossal power, that wave-driven ice ridge destroyed everything in its path and in a few places scrapped away the surface of the land down to bedrock. That was what we'd seen in Dingwall Harbour, where the polar bears had been feeding, and in Neil's Harbour—enormous ice ridges filled with the bodies and debris of absolute destruction. The scrapping effect had rearranged much of the shoreline, which we only saw once the ice had melted away.

She told the radio host that the earthquake that had caused the underwater landslide had happened in a place on the Grand Banks that had had only a few small earthquakes in recent years and never any big ones. She called it the 'epicentre' of the tsunami—the earthquake had caused a massive amount of sediment from an unstable shallow area to fall into deeper water. This epicentre was well north of the 1929 earthquake, about mid-way between Burgeo and Port aux Basques, just off the southwest coast of Newfoundland. It was not an area anyone had thought could produce a landslide of that size but nature, she pointed out, was always full of surprises.

I had to laugh at that, a real snort out loud: as if most Cape Bretoners didn't know that was true, just from living their lives!

The geologist also said that this devastating tsunami had been generated by a relatively small earthquake. This was something most geologists

150

knew was possible but it had been considered too unlikely to worry about. Any major tsunamis in the area, they had all believed, was likely to result from the same sequence of events as had happened in 1929: big earthquake, big underwater landslide, big tsunami. Small earthquake, big landslide, big tsunami just wasn't on their radar. This meant the magnitude 3.2 earthquake hadn't raised any red flags. As a consequence, they hadn't issued a tsunami warning until the first wave had already hit the south coast of Newfoundland. Halifax had a tsunami warning siren but Sydney and smaller communities on Cape Breton did not. The warning went out to the northern communities via television, marine radio and the internet but some folks either didn't hear it or it came too late to make a difference.

Of course, we all knew by that time that Burgeo and Port Aux Basques had been hit hard and fast. Because there was no ice cover on that coast, however, the damage was caused by the force of the water carried by the tsunami waves alone— as had been the case in 1929 on the Burin Peninsula. And as had happened in 1929, there had been no warning. But unlike 1929, there had not even been that odd retreat of water from the shore that signals a giant wave approaching—a spectacle

151

so profoundly odd that even if they don't understand what it means, makes people run for their lives. The inter-island ferry waiting at the dock in Port Aux Basques for that day's sailing to Sydney was not badly damaged but the ferry terminal was destroyed. A good many lives were lost all along that southwest coast of Newfoundland, I forget how many—a sickening number, I recall that much.

She went on to say that the north end of Cape Breton got hit especially hard because it was fairly close to the epicentre and the waves travelled in an almost-straight line to get there. The whole Aspy Bay area took a direct hit. Critically, much of that northern coastline was below 10 metres in elevation. That first ice-constrained wave exploded into the four shallow harbours of Aspy Bay and the two waves that followed did their own special brand of ice-shove damage. Because the area was so shallow, the water also took longer to drain out. Salt water soaked into the soil in some places, poisoning the ground and making recovery even harder. Highland folks need a garden, if only for potatoes.

Apparently, most of the communities along the east coast of Cape Breton, including Neil's Harbour, had suffered significantly less damage because the waves came in at an angle and high

152

ground stopped the waves before they'd gone as far inland. Also, many heard the marine warning or the roar of the breaking ice, which meant they'd seen the first wave approaching and had time to run.

Sydney hadn't been so lucky. The geologist said that the destruction in Sydney had been on such an unimaginable scale because it was like Dingwall in several respects: low-lying, built at the head of a long narrow harbour opening onto Cabot Strait, and hit pretty much head-on by the ice-laden waves. The big difference was that the tsunami had taken longer to get to Sydney, so there had been more time for warnings to go out. Those warnings had saved perhaps thousands of lives but unfortunately the alerts had no power to reduce the physical damage.

At the time of the tsunami—like many years in late March—Sydney Harbour had been covered in ice almost two metres thick, almost as thick as the ice out in the Sydney Bight area of Cabot Strait. In the weeks before the disaster, the ferry travelling to Newfoundland and back had needed an icebreaker escort to reach its North Sydney dock half way up the harbour. And then the wind change a few days before the disaster had compressed the ice even more. All that thick ice in the harbour simply increased the destructive power of the first tsunami wave—its energy was kept in check as it ran up the length of the ice-covered harbour and then exploded onshore as it reached the city centre. Ice blocks the size of trucks and weighing tons had been hurled ashore by the powerful surge of water.

The damage in the city was extensive and stretched for ten or twelve blocks beyond the shoreline in many areas—anything built on land lower than about 12 metres had been utterly destroyed. Halfway up the harbour, the community of North Sydney had been obliterated—that was the word she used—and the enormous steel ferry sitting at the dock was damaged beyond repair. It had been hit broadside by the wave, rolled over and eventually crushed by the ice in the middle, as if it were merely a beer can. The low-lying suburban communities along both sides of the harbour, as well as the coastal roads and highways used to access them, were wiped clean by the ice-shove.

While many lives were saved by the advanced warning over the entire area of Sydney Harbour, hundreds of people were simply too far from higher ground to save themselves by the time they realized they were in danger. If they hadn't heard any of the official alarms or been alerted by neighbours, their only warning had been the deafening roar of the approaching first wave. The geologist said if it hadn't been a Sunday morning, when the downtown office towers were empty, the loss of life could have been in the tens of thousands rather than a few hundred.

Then she'd played a tape of a Sydney resident, who'd been out walking his dog that morning, talk about what he'd seen from a spot of high ground above the city. He'd heard the roar of the ice breaking as the first tsunami wave came up the harbour and stood to watch. It gave me goosebumps then to hear him describe what he saw and heard, and now I have them again just remembering his voice—quiet, like he was talking in church, recalling a nightmare that had scared him witless.

"The noise was deafening. It started like distant thunder but as the wave barreled down the harbour, the roar became terrifying. As the rolling mound of ice hit the shore, chunks the size of buses flew through the air. Then it became a wall— a wall of relentless ice. Everything simply disappeared under it. It just kept coming, devouring city block after city block. Nothing could stop it. When it came to a tall building, the tower would jump and topple as if a rug had been pulled out from under it—it knocked out the bottom level of the building and the rest flew into the air and fell over, exploding on impact. And so on, for all the other office and apartment towers it touched. I could see people running for higher ground but couldn't hear them screaming—the din from the ice and the crashing buildings was too loud. It was absolutely surreal, like watching a disaster movie with fabulous special effects. Except that one of the apartment towers I watched explode was where my parents lived."

The geologist lady turned the tape off and said the man had gone on to assist in the rescue but had suffered severe psychological trauma later on. It had been worse, she said, for people like him. They kept replaying in their heads what they'd seen. A recurring nightmare—PTSD, she called it. Not just in Sydney but all over Cape Breton, people who had survived were struggling with their sanity.

Now that I think of it, maybe that's what happened to Logan. Between watching the tsunami wipe out the town he'd lived in all his life plus the sight of his brother's body half-eaten by a polar bear, something in his mind must have snapped. I guess two nightmare images to replay were too much for him.

At the end of her interview, the geologist pointed out the critical folly of Sydney having built its two coal-powered electrical plants on the coastal lowlands either side of the harbour. These had been the first structures destroyed by the surging water and ice blocks hurled ashore by the tsunami. If it hadn't been daylight already, the loss of power would have plunged the city into darkness a good fifteen minutes before the first wave reached the area where most people lived. As it was, Sydney's survivors were left without electrical power for many months following the disaster. With both power plants gone and the nearby coal mine that had supplied the fuel also destroyed, the citizens of Sydney faced a depressingly slow job of cleaning up and rebuilding their city.

I don't know how they managed. I simply left. With my boat gone and my good friends lost, my heart was no longer into staying around to see Neil's Harbour through its recovery. I left my house to neighbours who had nowhere to live, just as Logan had done. I flew over to Newfoundland and stayed at John's place. At first it was only going to be for awhile but at some point, my visit had turned into a permanent arrangement. I slowly fixed up a big storage shed he had out back into a livable cabin and workshop, and got solitary comfort making furniture from wood salvaged from the wreckage of the tsunami that eventually became strewn around the Gulf. It was my small act of rebuilding, I guess, something I could do until I couldn't do anything at all anymore—at which point I ended up here in the home. There were no more trips to the ice after the tsunami. But I didn't miss it. It was like I'd been cured of an addiction I hadn't known I'd had—snapped out of it, it seemed to me, by that polar bear's defiant gaze. You know, I still see his eyes in my dreams sometimes, even after all these years.

Having said it all out loud now, I can see why I hadn't told the story years ago. It wasn't fear of being ridiculed by those who doubted I'd come face-to-face with a polar bear that held me back, it was how I'd treated Izzy. And that is what has haunted me. The story reflected badly on me and I was too proud to admit it.

After the tsunami, I knew I no longer had what it took to go out on the ice. I was OK with that. I'd come to terms with the fact that the ice in the Gulf had transformed—where once it had been a joyfully challenging place to hunt seals, now it was home to a fast and fearless predator that hid in the shadows and silently stalked its prey. No sealer would ever really be safe walking the ice of the Gulf again. Even a hunter who knew the ways of the ice could at any time become the hunted. I was not too proud to admit I didn't want to work in a place ruled by polar bears as well as weather. That hadn't been the problem.

What I hadn't been able to accept was that as Izzy's teacher, I'd let her down so badly. I was disappointed with myself. No, that's still not entirely honest. Not just disappointed—ashamed. I'd taken on the job to teach her but had refused to share what may have been the most important lesson of all. Even though I'd only learned it myself a few moments before, that was no real excuse for staying silent.

I'd told Izzy how much I'd learned from the stories other sealers and fishermen had told about deadly and near-deadly experiences, pointed out how important knowing about these mistakes made by others were to staying alive on the ice. I'd taken so much pride in being honest and straight with her then but when it really counted, I'd pretended a need to shield her from a gruesome sight and held my tongue. An inexcusably selfish act that was, to refuse to share what I'd learned. And she knew what I'd done, which made it even worse. I was deeply ashamed.

I should have warned her—prepare to be humbled.

*****

CPSIA information can be obtained
at www.ICGtesting.com
Printed in the USA
LVHW082203160221
679287LV00013BA/2089